Readers love
ANDREW GREY

Heartward

"Whoooo. This one hits you right in the feels. Man."
—Love Bytes

"I really enjoyed this emotional and well written full length story."
—Long and Short Reviews

Pulling Strings

"I don't have any problem recommending Pulling Strings. It's a good, solid mystery/romance, and if that's up your alley, you should definitely pick this one up."
—Joyfully Jay

"I love it when a story can cause me to keep guessing until end and make it plausible at the same time. Very well done."
—Gay Book Reviews

Twice Baked

"This a great second chance romance novel... There is loads of charm and romance."
—MM Good Book Reviews

"A fun and flirty story I enjoyed and I believe you will, too."
—Bayou Book Junkie

More praise for
ANDREW GREY

Heart Unbroken

"If you have read Mr. Grey's books before, then you don't need a review to know you are in for a story that will touch you in so many ways."

—Paranormal Romance Guild

Survive and Conquer

"…if you don't read this, you're missing out on a hell of a book. The way it's written is absolutely amazing and I'm glad I got the chance to read it."

—Love Bytes

"The emotions are overflowing, the characters are very deep and complex, it was a wild journey to get to know them and their motivations."

—MM Good Book Reviews

Published by DREAMSPINNER PRESS
www.dreamspinnerpress.com

Published by DREAMSPINNER PRESS
www.dreamspinnerpress.com

HARD ROAD
Back

ANDREW GREY

Published by
DREAMSPINNER PRESS

5032 Capital Circle SW, Suite 2, PMB# 279, Tallahassee, FL 32305-7886 USA
www.dreamspinnerpress.com

Hard Road Back
© 2020 Andrew Grey

Cover Art
© 2020 Kanaxa
Cover content is for illustrative purposes only and any person depicted on the cover is a model.

Trade Paperback ISBN: 978-1-64405-613-4
Digital ISBN: 978-1-64405-612-7
Library of Congress Control Number: 2019955837
Trade Paperback published May 2020
v. 1.0

Printed in the United States of America
∞
This paper meets the requirements of
ANSI/NISO Z39.48-1992 (Permanence of Paper).

To Dominic,
who always has my back and supports me no matter what.

CHAPTER 1

I KNEW some of his secrets, but by no means all of them. Lord knows there's no man alive, other than Scarborough himself, who knows all of those. He keeps shit to himself better than any man I've ever met, and that's saying a hell of a lot, being a cowboy—well, of sorts.... All in all, you meet a whole hell of a lot of guys with chips on their shoulders, and even more keeping stuff to themselves. I have been friends of a sort with him for fifteen years now, and sometimes he still seems like a stranger. And yet, I think I can see a little boy behind the bluest, biggest, most perfect eyes God ever put on a man. But I know I shouldn't go there because that is a road I should not go down. It's laced with more potholes than Scarborough's driveway... and that's saying something.

Normally I would try not to think about Scarborough Croughton, at least as much as I can, but his ranch borders my small piece of property, so I get to see him more than just about anyone. This morning, either by luck or by a visit from the devil, the damned phone rang just as I was getting out of bed... and I'm not going to say I was dreaming about that cantankerous pain in the ass.

"Yeah, Scarborough, what do you need?" I checked the clock, and it was just after five in the morning. I should be getting up anyway, but it would have been nice to get another few minutes of sleep.

"I got a problem and I need yer help," he said. No indication of what the problem was, just those few words. Sometimes I

1

wondered if Scarborough figured he only got to say so many words in his entire life, and being as he was determined to live until doomsday, he had to use as few as possible.

"I'm supposed to be at Sandy Reynold's place today. I can come over for about an hour, but then I got to go see her."

Scarborough humphed. "'Kay."

I could tell he was about to hang up, and I groaned silently in my head. "Let me get dressed and I'll be over. You got coffee on?" I hoped to the ever-loving gods. "I'll be there as soon as I can."

"Thanks." The line went dead.

I shuffled off to the bathroom and scoured my face with a razor, thankful I didn't cut myself all to hell, used the toilet, and finished my morning routine before dressing and heading right to the door.

Beau met me there, tail wagging, eyes bright, looking up at me as though he knew I was heading out. I checked that he had food in his dish and water in the bowl. He was a good dog and pretty much ate when he was hungry. As soon as I opened the door, Beau took off to make his morning rounds. That dog had a sixth sense, I was pretty sure. He ran to the small barn to check on the horses, waiting for me. I let my babies out into their paddocks and made sure they had plenty of water for the day, scratching noses and saying hello. Each of those beauties was a horse I had rescued and rehabilitated in one way or another, and each had a story. But I was in too much of a hurry to think about that right now.

I headed to the truck, and Beau jumped in and went right to his spot, with his front legs on the arm of the passenger's side door, his tongue hanging out as I started the engine. As soon as the cool air started blowing out of the vents, he got down, his nose in the stream, his mouth open.

The trip to Scarborough's took all of five minutes, but walking would've been a real pain and taken much longer. I pulled into the drive and noticed that I didn't get shook all to hell. He must have graded the thing at some point. He came out of the house as I slowed, and by the time I was out of the truck, he'd caught up to me with mismatched mugs in each hand.

"Oh thank God," I said as I took the mug and sipped what I knew was the strongest damned coffee in the state of Wyoming.

"Over here," Scarborough said, and I let him lead. I was going to have to find out for myself what was happening. But that didn't mean I couldn't enjoy the view, at least for a few minutes.

Scarborough had grown up on this land. That much everyone in town knew. His mom had passed in a bad way, and as far as I knew, his father was distant. I'd met him fifteen years ago when he'd moved in down the road. Losing his mom to a drunken truck driver was not a prescription for good emotional health, as far as I was concerned.

"Did you pick up a new horse?" I asked as we got closer to the paddocks. Beau stopped, plopping his butt on a small patch of scraggly grass, watching, his tongue lolling, but coming no closer. We turned the corner of the low barn, and I stopped dead in my tracks. A horse as black as midnight looked back at me with some of the wildest eyes I had ever seen.

I motioned to Scarborough to stay where he was as I took small steps forward. "That's a good boy," I said, letting the breeze carry the words to him, making him strain to hear. "My gosh, you are stunning." He stayed still, but the wildness and fear in those huge brown eyes pulled at my heart. What the fuck had happened to this magnificent horse to make him that way? "I'm not going to hurt you. I just want to see you." I didn't reach for him and just spoke a string of nonsense words.

There was intelligence behind those eyes and the way they held my gaze. The horse began breathing more heavily, a front leg shaking, and Scarborough took a step back and then another. Finally the horse turned, raced to the far side of the paddock, stopped, and turned again to watch.

"Where did you find him?" I asked.

"Auction," Scarborough answered.

I sipped from my mug, completely surprised. That made no sense at all. Not that Scarborough didn't go to auctions—he did. The man had a good sense about horses, and an even better one about anything profitable. Scarborough could make money, and, well, he didn't spend it unless he thought he could get more. It was just that simple. I've known penny-pinchers in my life, but Scarborough made Abe Lincoln scream bloody murder before he spent anything at all. "Why did you buy him? You know there's the possibility that he will never be of any use to anyone." But damn, he was stunning as all hell, nonetheless. "What's his name?" I turned to Scarborough just in time to see him roll his eyes.

"Whoever had him before actually named him Black Beauty." Scarborough made a face. "I hate it." He usually didn't do that sort of thing, and I liked seeing Scarborough's playful side. "I'm going to rename him, but I don't know what yet."

"Maybe he'll suggest a name," I offered, and Scarborough nodded but grew quiet once again. That was his usual way, and I was more than used to it. With Scarborough, you had to read between the lines quite a bit. And sometimes there weren't even lines—you simply had to guess.

He lifted the mug slowly to his lips. "I thought you could fix him, and then I would use him for stud. His bloodlines are amazing, and… look at him."

Was that softness I saw around Scarborough's eyes, even for a second? I wasn't sure, and any tenderness that was there didn't last too long.

"I'll pay you."

I nearly took a step back. Those words never crossed Scarborough's lips. I wanted to put my hand over my chest to check that I wasn't going to have a heart attack, or run to town to see the doc because I wanted to make sure I wasn't hearing shit. "You sure?" There was so much fear and pain there that I wasn't sure anyone could ever get through it, but for Scarborough I was willing to try. And if it was important enough for him to offer to pay me, then I would definitely do my best.

Scarborough nodded and mumbled an assent.

"Okay, I'll do what I can. I'll text you over an agreement that states my terms and rates, like with anyone else. If you agree, you sign and return it, and I'll get started as soon as I can. Don't let anyone near him for now, and feed and water him yourself. Let him associate both things with you. It will help. And for God's sake, don't stomp or make any sharp noises around him."

"Huh?"

I rolled my eyes. "Just be nice to him, okay? I know you can do that." I smiled.

Scarborough humphed but then nodded, and a ghost of a smile formed on his lips. "I will. I'm better with horses than people." He turned to look at the horse once again. "Just make him better and stop the cycle of pain that's going through his head right now."

I blinked because I honestly wasn't sure if he was truly talking about the horse or himself.

Beau ambled over, and I patted his head. Nodding, I checked my watch and headed toward the truck. "I'll send over the agreement, and I can start in a few days. I'll probably work with him in the mornings before my other jobs. So have the coffee on." I waved and pulled open the door. Beau jumped in, and I climbed into the truck and headed back down the drive.

I wondered about Scarborough for the next half hour as I drove to Sandy's place. I pulled in and parked in my usual spot in front of the house. Her pack of dogs came over, barking and wagging their tails. I let Beau out, and he greeted his old friends with happy barks, and soon he was off with the pack.

"Martin, you're late," Sandy said as she stepped out on the porch. "I got coffee and some breakfast for you. Come on inside

5

and eat, and then we can get to work." She motioned, and I wiped off my boots before stepping inside.

"Sorry. Scarborough called this morning and said he needed my help."

She scoffed. "Looking for free work?" She, like a lot of the people in town, was not particularly a fan of my neighbor. They had all, at one time or other, been on the cheap end of his ways, and that made them skeptical, so they tended to avoid him if possible. Not that I could exactly blame them.

"No. He bought a horse at auction that he needs me to work with." I sat down at the kitchen table, which had seen at least three generations of her family, the scuffs and marks a history of family meals.

"For free?" She brought over a plate and set it in front of me, along with a glass of juice and some more coffee. Only hers was danged good. No one made coffee like Sandy.

"Nope. He said he'd pay me." I took a bite as she fumbled with her chair.

"Well, I'll be damned." She sat down and sipped her coffee. "I know it was hard when his mom died, but something changed him. Not that I blame him for being hurt after she was gone, but he never seemed to spring back all the way. He did for a while… and then… he didn't."

"Everyone thinks it was the accident."

She nodded and seemed thoughtful. "It could have been, though I think it was more than that. There's something else that happened. But I don't know what it is. I think only Scarborough does, and he isn't going to talk about it to anyone." She sighed. "Every time I have to deal with him, I try to remember the way he was and not the skinflint he is now, but it's damned hard."

"Mom, bad word," her five-year-old daughter said as she toddled up.

Sandy lifted her onto her lap. Megan was Sandy's surprise baby, and no child was loved more. Sandy and Joe had never thought they could have kids and had long before given up. Then surprise, along came Megan—about the time that Joe took up and then off with June Mather, the former mayor's wife. What a mess that was for all of them. Thankfully Joe had had the sense to get the hell out of town before he got run out of it.

"I'm sorry," she said gently, and Megan cuddled close. She was dressed but seemed a little clingy.

"Did you sleep good?" I asked, and she shook her head.

"She has a case of the sniffles. The doctor says she'll be fine in a day or so, but right now she just wants her mom as much as possible." Sandy sat back and let Megan rest against her while I ate the feast she had made for me. "Why would Scarborough buy a horse at auction with a lot of problems?" Sandy asked. "That seems like a lot more trouble than it's worth for him." There was a lot left unsaid in that statement.

"I wondered the same thing. He wants me to calm him down enough that he can be used for stud." I savored the eggs, which were perfect sunny-side up, and picked up a piece of bacon. Megan turned toward me, and I offered her a piece. She smiled and took it. "The thing is, he's stunning beyond belief. The coloring and his gait. Just seeing him move was a thing of beauty, but he's filled with soul-deep fear. I have no idea how anyone got him into a trailer for transport. They must have drugged him, which can lead to a whole set of problems." I finished the last of the food, drank the juice, and wanted to sit back and close my eyes, but there was work to do. And Sandy, while she always gave me breakfast, wasn't paying me to sit around and jaw.

"That's a real shame. Things like that are only going to make it worse for him… and you in the end." She put Megan down and took care of the dishes. "Do you think you can help?"

"I'll try." I thanked her for breakfast and went out to spend the rest of the morning working with one of her new horses that had picked up some bad habits. But for some reason, Scarborough and his horse stayed in my mind. Yes, what Scarborough had said might have made sense, but it was so unlike him. Scarborough bought horses when he thought he could make money. He didn't buy horses that needed rehab, because of the additional cost and the uncertainty. That kept me thinking about what Scarborough was actually up to.

AFTER THE morning at Sandy's, I spent the afternoon at a few other clients' before stopping at the house to check on things. Beau ran around like he had been gone for days, checking out his spots and making sure all the animals that might come roaming knew this was his. The silly dog did it every single time we went away, even if it was for a few hours.

"Hey, Dad," I said when my father came out of the barn. "What are you doing?"

"Just looking," he answered. My dad was the quintessential cowboy, in his jeans, boots, hat, and one of the buckles he'd won when he rode broncs. That was how he met my mother. Dad always said that she was a buckle bunny and that he'd had to fight off dozens of guys to win her attention. Every time he said it, Mom would wink, which meant she was letting Dad have his fantasy. The truth, from Mom, was that she saw him and wasn't going to make it too easy to be caught. I believed her. "Ted had a horse that he needs to sell, and I want to buy it. I have a buyer out near Casper for it, but they aren't ready for him until next month. My barn is full, but…."

"I got space," I told him. "Go ahead and make the deal. I got your back." I loved that I could help my dad out every once in a while. I'd bought the place because it was next door to my folks. That way I could be close if they needed me, and yet have a place of my own. The plan was that I would eventually inherit the entire ranch, and my idea was to put everything together.

"It's too good a deal to pass up. This horse is a beaut, and Ted needs the cash bad, so I made him a fair offer, and he took it. This guy from Casper is looking to pay top dollar." Dad grinned. He was literally a horse trader from way back. Dad raised some horses on the ranch, as well as running some cattle, but he really made his money trading. It was in his blood, just like horses and what they needed was in mine. "You coming for dinner? Your mom wanted me to ask."

I was about to answer when Scarborough's truck turned into the drive. He pulled to a stop and lowered the window. "The new horse is going crazy. Can you come now? I don't know what to do."

"Go on. I'll do the evening feed while I'm here." Dad was already heading back toward the barn, so I hopped into Scarborough's truck. Beau instantly barked his head off, and I opened the door to let him jump in.

"What is he doing?" I asked as we rode.

"Stamping and rearing and braying constantly. I tried to see if anything was in the paddock, but I can't get close enough." The concern in his voice rang like a bell. "I don't want him to hurt himself, and if it goes on for much longer, he's going to." As soon as he hit the road, Scarborough floored it, whipping down the street and only slowing when he approached his drive, and we skidded a little nonetheless.

As soon as I opened the door, a wave of fear washed over me. The air was palpable with it. As much as I wanted to run, I forced myself to walk to the paddock, where Black Beauty had nearly exhausted himself in his panicked frenzy. His coat shimmered with sweat and his mouth foamed a little. "Scarborough, go around the back and open the gate. Give him an out and let's see if he'll take it. That area is bigger, but fenced, right?"

"Yeah. But there are other horses in there."

"Get them out, now," I said, and Scarborough hurried away. I started talking softly, trying to calm the horse, but he wasn't having it. Black Beauty was too worked up to allow for that. I still attempted to distract him and at one point had him still and

9

breathing deeply, but his eyes were wild. I tried to keep him calm, but then he reared again and nearly clocked the fence on his way down. "Open the gate," I called, and Scarborough swung the large gate open with a loud squeak.

The sound drew the horse's attention, and he turned and raced through to the roomier paddock, then stopped in the center. From where I stood, I saw him still breathing heavily, but at least the frantic stomping and jumping had ended.

Scarborough closed the paddock gate and locked it. "What the fuck was all that about?" he asked as he came over.

"Go get him some hay, and make sure there is plenty of water for him. I want to check out this enclosure." There was something strange going on, and I was determined to get to the bottom of it. "Keep plenty of distance." I knew we were damned lucky the horse hadn't keeled over from a heart attack. Horses are strangely fragile creatures, powerful and beautiful, but also delicate. I wondered how many times during his tirade Black Beauty had come close to breaking a leg.

I climbed the fence, dropped into the paddock, and walked the area. It was clear to me that Scarborough hadn't used the paddock in a while. Not that it was in bad repair, but the grass inside was longer and hadn't been eaten down. Anyway, I knew I had to be careful.

"Find anything?" Scarborough asked.

I shook my head, then paused. A snake lay in the grass. I stilled instantly and backed away, watching it, but the snake didn't move. I went back, grabbed a shovel, and approached once again. The snake was in the same position. I slammed it with the shovel, expecting a pile of guts. Scooping it up, I carried what should have been a carcass to Scarborough and tossed it at him. He jumped back, shrieking as the rubber snake bounced off the fencing.

"What the hell?"

"Exactly. Someone put this in the paddock." I continued around and thought I'd found another. I was about to scoop it up when the familiar rattle sent a zing up my spine. I pulled back and the sound stopped. "Good God."

"What?" Scarborough hurried over, and I put up my hand to stop him.

"There's a live one in here too," I called out.

Scarborough had had more than enough experience with snakes, and he wrangled the little slitherer into a bag and got rid of it. The situation was beyond crazy as far as I was concerned.

"What the hell did you do to someone that they would put a snake in one of your paddocks?" Yeah, I knew Scarborough was cheap, but as far as I knew, he didn't cheat anyone and paid his bills. It wasn't like he was cruel or mean, just skinflinty.

"You really think someone put that in here?" he asked.

"Well," I said, pointing, "someone put the rubber one in here. Think about it. They got a live snake, put it in here, and then added the rubber one, so the horse thought they were all around him and went out of his mind." Everyone knew that horses didn't like snakes. The reaction was pretty common. But to have an already wild horse and to add a snake to its paddock was a recipe for disaster. Thank God it had been diverted.

Scarborough bent down and lifted the remains of yet another rubber snake that had been trounced to pieces. "I think you're right." He tossed the remains to the side of the paddock. I tried to read what he was thinking, but like so much of the time, Scarborough was stoic as hell. Still, his posture seemed more rigid than usual, and he kept looking around.

"Who might want to get even with you or cause trouble?" I knew Scarborough didn't have disgruntled employees, because it was just him here on the ranch. He did whatever he needed himself because help would require him to pay them.

He stood still, and I took a few seconds just to watch him and wait for some sort of response. Scarborough had spent his entire life outside, working hard, and it showed in every muscle in his body. I had been to the city and seen guys whose bodies came from gyms, with their perfect bubble butts and chests that seemed to sprout plates. But Scarborough wasn't like that. His was a body of a life of hard work, with corded muscle and a compact strength from lifting bales of hay and splitting enough wood to heat the house for the winter.

His jeans were old and maybe a little threadbare in places, hugging his legs and backside like a second skin. I knew it was a bad idea to be looking at my neighbor that way, but what the hell? He seemed lost in his own thoughts for a few minutes, and I sure as hell could let my own mind wander. It didn't hurt anything, and I didn't have any illusions that Scarborough was going to suddenly wake up and realize that I was his dream guy. He wasn't going to open his arms and change his ways at the drop of a hat—or because of a single longing look across a paddock. That sort of thing was not Scarborough Croughton in the least.

"I don't know," he finally answered, then turned away, going about cleaning up the rubber snakes and checking the last of the paddock.

Not that it was likely that he was going to be able to put Black Beauty in this paddock. He was going to remember, and it would only make him nervous again. At least he seemed to be eating now and drinking some, which meant that the panic in him was over. But this afternoon's incident had made my job a little harder, and I was going to need all the patience I could muster to try to help that horse—and Scarborough, for that matter.

"Keep an eye on him, and I'll get the paperwork sent over right away. I should have some time in a few days."

He nodded. "I'll do my best to try to keep him calm and see if maybe he'll forget some of this incident."

That was our only hope to get him past whatever trauma had left the horse so full of fear that he'd spook like that. I also wondered what could have happened to Scarborough to make him withdraw from everyone the way he had too. I wondered which of the two would be easier to understand in the end.

CHAPTER 2

"YOUR DAD said that Scarborough was having trouble with a horse?" my mother said as she worked in her kitchen. That part of the house was very much her domain, and it was exactly the way she wanted it. When she had decided that she wanted the wall over the sink removed so she could see into the rest of the house and my dad had balked, he came home one day to find my mom with a Sawzall in her hand, cutting out the section she wanted gone and telling Dad to clean up the mess and finish the job. We were lucky she hadn't cut any of the wiring or plumbing, but Mom got her kitchen the way she wanted it.

"Yes. He's one walking ball of fear and equestrian anxiety." I sighed, took the plate of bruschetta from the counter, and put it on the coffee table in the living room, Beau following the food but making no move to take anything. He was too well trained. Mom knew that Dad and I would need a snack before dinner. "I really don't know why he bought him. It isn't like Scarborough to buy a horse or anything else that will require that kind of work and expense to recoup his investment."

Mom shook her head. "That boy is deeper than anybody gives him credit for." She went back to making dinner, and I turned, hoping she would elaborate. "I thought I'd make some of my roast beef for dinner. They had it on sale at Hansen's this week, and I know you and your father love it." We did, but that wasn't the point. She had changed her own subject, and that was the end of it.

"Mom," I tried coaxing, and she turned to me with eyes as thoughtful as ever, her lips curling upward. "You don't get to drop something like that and then back off."

She shrugged. "He has nice eyes."

I scoffed. "You know, he does. Nice rear end too." I had to throw in the last part, and Mom huffed and flashed me an annoyed frown.

"Do you like Scarborough that way?" she asked. "You know it's okay if you do."

I chuckled. "Mom, can you really see the two of us together? Me and Scarborough…." The idea seemed preposterous and yet…. I pushed the notion out of my head. "Mom, you have got to be kidding."

She gave me this knowing look and didn't say anything. I inhaled, intent to get at whatever idea was taking root in her head. But then I snapped my mouth shut, figuring my mother would just dig in her heels, and the notion that might be fleeting now would suddenly become firmly embedded in her psyche—and then it would be like pulling molars to get her to let it go.

"Give it up, son," my dad said softly as he came in from down the hallway and joined me in the living room. "You do not want your mother deciding she wants to play matchmaker. You remember your cousin Claudia." He made sure to speak loud enough so Mom heard.

"She and Lorenzo were perfect for each other, and then she went and married Jordan. That lasted two years and now they've split up, and I still think she should date Lorenzo." Mom went back to her cooking as I popped one of her bruschetta into my mouth, moaning at the garlicy tomato perfection. "He's still single, and he was asking about her the last time I saw him." Mom rarely ever gave up on anything, especially when she thought she was right.

"I don't think Claudia is ready to date anyone," I said.

Dad leaned forward. "Why are you continuing this?"

I lowered my voice and shifted closer to Dad. "If she's going on about Claudia, then she'll leave my love life alone." Not that I had much of one. It wasn't like there were many gay people in Red Rock, but that wasn't going to stop my mother. And if she got it in her head that Scarborough and I should be together simply because we were the only gay people within spitting distance of each other, then my life was going to descend into my mother's manipulative version of matchmaking hell.

Dad snickered softly. "Good idea."

"What are you two whispering about in there?" Mom asked.

"Nothing, dear," Dad said gently. "He and I are talking about the horse that I'm going to put in his barn for a month or so. It's going to require some special care." That was the first I had heard about that. "There's steeplechasing in his lineage, and I think the new owners are going to try to train him. I'm not sure, but this guy is a real gem." Dad patted my leg.

"Do you want him exercised?" I wasn't that type of rider, but I knew how to keep a horse in shape.

"Yes. He's going to need regular exercise and things. But the biggest thing is to make sure that he's well fed, and before delivery, we're going to need to brush and groom him up so he looks his absolute showy best." Dad never cheated anyone, and there had been times when he didn't get what he was expecting—that was part of the business. But Dad also knew that to get top dollar for a horse, it should look its best, and apparently this horse could be a chance for Dad to make a good share of his year.

Mom came into the room, took a bite of bruschetta, and sat on the sofa. "Dinner is in the oven." She turned to me, and I wondered what was behind her eyes. "Scarborough will be here in half an hour. It's been a long time since he's had a home-cooked meal, and he was looking skinny the last time I saw him."

There was no way I could protest, even though I thought I knew what she was up to.

I sat back and tried to seem casual. I had honestly never thought of Scarborough as anything other than a friend... of sorts. He and I didn't go out on the town or spend nights drinking together. Scarborough would never do something like that. If he wanted to drink, he bought what he wanted and drank at home. We also didn't go out to the movies or take trips together. Scarborough was the kind of friend who called me when he needed something, and I did the same. We could rely on each other.

But, damn it all, now that my mother had put the idea into my head that Scarborough might be someone more interesting than that, my mind kept going back to how he looked, standing tall, with his broad shoulders and narrow waist, leaning on the first fence rail, looking over the paddock. And don't get me started on how he looked on a horse. I had seen him like that so many times, and the man was a dream when riding. Okay, there had been times when I wondered what it would feel like to have those long legs of his wrapped around my hips and my hands on his shoulders, his eyes half-lidded as I drove him to heaven. God, Scarborough never said much, but I wondered what he would be like in bed, and—I slowly crossed my legs as my jeans grew a little tighter. I definitely needed to think about something else or I was going to fucking embarrass myself in front of my mother, right here in her living room, and it would be all her damned fault.

"How are the kids you're working with at the center?" I asked, very much needing to change the subject. Mom volunteered down at the local children's center. Before she'd retired, Mom taught kindergarten for nearly forty years. Now she spent some of her time volunteering with kids who needed extra help in school or with just basic developmental and motor skills.

She clicked her tongue softly. "Some of these kids could do with a lot more parenting. There's nothing wrong with them other than the fact that their mom or dad doesn't work with them. One little boy learned his ABCs in three days. His mom never bothered to review them with him. I know parents can't stay home and have to work, but they still need to work with their children. It's so sad sometimes."

I knew there was a lot more than Mom was talking about. But with this, Mom was discreet. A lot of the time if she told stories, it would be possible to figure out who she was talking about. Red Rock just wasn't that big a town, and I knew almost everyone, at least by association.

"It's good that you can help them," I told her.

She nodded and ate another of her snacks before repositioning the plate near me and my father and away from her. Mom had gotten this idea lately that she needed to lose weight. She had never been heavy, and when she went to the doctor and he told her she had put on five pounds, she was determined to get it off once again. "I love what I do, but some of these kids deserve more than what they're getting as far as parents are concerned."

"Not all of them can have you for a mom." I smiled, and she grinned.

A vehicle pulled into the drive, the lights illuminating the curtains. "That must be Scarborough." Mom stood and answered the door, with Beau right behind her. He sat to see who it was, probably wondering if he was going to get more attention out of the deal. "I'm glad you could join us." She hugged Scarborough and stepped back so he could come inside.

Sometimes I forgot how well Scarborough could clean up. His black hair shone, and he had on new jeans and a white button-down shirt. He looked downright respectable. And when he smiled at Mom, I sort of wished he'd flash those perfect teeth at me every once in a while. Not that I was ready to admit that to anyone other than myself.

"Thank you for inviting me. I was about to make myself some sandwiches and then try to make a dent in the growing list of chores."

"Nonsense. You can't work all the time, and you need some good home cooking just as much as the rest of us." Mom closed the door so she didn't let any more of the cool air out and motioned to the chairs. Dad and I had stood, and we both shook hands with Scarborough before sitting once again.

"How's the horse?" I asked.

"He's been quiet since we moved him, though still jumpy as hell. I hope you can do something to help him, or otherwise he isn't going to be good for anything. And no one is going to want to breed their mares to a crazy horse." He pursed his lips and slowly sat down. I passed him the plate, and he took one of Mom's nibbles. "I don't know what I was thinking. I sat in that auction, and all I could see was how stunning he was, so I bought him."

"He is great-looking. Do you think they had him drugged or something at the sale? The horse I saw was never going to stand for being around that many people without going out of his mind."

Scarborough shrugged. "I didn't think so at the time, but it's possible. Harrington's doesn't go in for that sort of thing, so it would never have occurred to me." He sat at the edge of his seat, like he expected to jump up at any second.

"If you like, I can take a look at him," Dad offered. Few people were as respected as my dad when it came to horses.

"Thank you." Scarborough finally sat back. "I'm not sure what's going on."

Mom went into the kitchen. I heard her setting the table and getting ready for dinner. I should probably have gone to help her, but I didn't want to leave Scarborough.

I explained to my dad about the snake in the paddock, along with the rubber ones. "What could someone be trying to pull? I mean, it wasn't like they were hiding what they were doing very well. They left rubber snakes, for God's sake. A clutch of rattlers could get into any paddock, especially one that hasn't been used in a while. But not rubber ones."

"Someone has it in for your horse," Dad said. "And they wanted you to know it." He leaned forward. "At the auction, were you bidding against anyone in particular?"

Scarborough shook his head.

"Did you pay a lot for him?" I asked, curious, though I thought I already knew the answer. Scarborough was the kind of man to jump after a bargain, but he wasn't one to overpay for anything.

"No," Scarborough said, his eyes flicking to me and then to my dad. "There was no one interested in him, and I bought on an opening bid. There weren't many people there."

I could tell there was something whirring in Scarborough's head, but he wasn't talking about whatever he was thinking.

"Did anything unusual happen?" Dad asked. If I didn't know better, I'd have figured he was driving at something, but I'd be damned if I could figure out what it was. "Were you offered anything after the sale or approached about anything?"

Scarborough shrugged.

"Okay, well, we're going to have to keep an eye out."

I leaned forward. "Is something going on that you aren't telling us? Someone working that auction?" It had been done before. Someone with influence putting the word out that a horse was off-limits or not to bid. It was rare, and in the age of the internet and online sales, hard to do. But in the old days, sometimes slipping a few bucks to the auction house and a few words of warning were enough to sink a sale or to ensure there were no other buyers. But in a place like Harrington's? That was hard to believe. They had been an upstanding livestock auction house for years, and had a stellar reputation all around. That sort of thing wasn't their style at all.

"Not that I've heard," Dad explained, and my dad usually heard rumors and scuttlebutt faster than just about anyone. His contacts were far and wide, and little in the horse business didn't cross his ears at one time or another. "But I'll do my usual listening and see if there are any whispers." Dad got out of his chair and went into the kitchen, where I could hear him and Mom whispering and then a soft giggle.

"Kyle," she whispered breathily, and I did my best to ignore them. I loved that my mom and dad loved each other. My dad was often stoic and held his cards close to his vest when it came to business—and I often felt that my dad always figured that as soon as he stepped out of the house, he was conducting business. But at home with my mom, he was affectionate. He had even been that way when I was a kid. I always knew that my dad loved me, no matter what.

When I pulled my mind out of my thoughts, I found Scarborough staring at me, and then he glanced toward the kitchen and back to me. He seemed to be trying to puzzle out something important.

"Are they always like that?" he whispered.

I shrugged and then nodded. It really was no big deal. "Mom and Dad were a love-at-first-sight sort of thing." My dad used to tell me the story of how he and Mom met. It was a kind of family legend. "Dad was riding rodeo, and Mom used to follow it. She still does to a degree. Dad likes to say he caught the best lady there was. But I think the truth is that he saw her at a rodeo and fell in love with her. She apparently thought he was handsome too. But she stayed away, and when Dad came around after her, she was determined she wasn't going to be caught. Right, Mom?" I added when she came in the room.

"That's right. I knew if he caught me too soon that I wasn't going to keep his attention. So I strung him out for a year. I let him write to me and I wrote him back, but…." She grinned. "I knew there was not going to be any ring-a-ding-ding unless I had a diamond on my finger."

"She put me through my paces," Dad added, coming up behind her. "But I was determined, and after I won big a few times, I bought the ring and made sure to marry her fast so no one could steal her away." As craggy and gruff as Dad could be sometimes, the gentleness in his eyes when he looked at Mom was something I always remembered seeing.

A timer sounded in the kitchen, and Mom swatted at Dad lightly before going to take care of it. Dad followed.

"That's nice," Scarborough said, and I waited for him to say something about his own family, but he just sighed.

"It is. What were your folks like?" I asked.

Now it was his turn to shrug. "Not like them. I think they hated each other most of the time. I hardly remember them being in the same room unless they were fighting about something. Usually money." He grew quiet once more, and Mom came in to tell us that dinner was ready.

I had never met Scarborough's dad. I knew Scarborough had grown up somewhere in Nebraska and had left home when he was eighteen or so. He'd worked as a farmhand, and from what I'd been able to piece together over the years, he saved every cent he could so he could have a place of his own, one that he could call home. I remember about five years ago, Scarborough asked me to watch his place and care for the animals while he went back for his mom's funeral. He'd been gone for a few weeks. There had not been any further talk about his mom and dad until tonight.

I let Scarborough go first, and Mom fussed over him with her roast, which smelled like beefy heaven, and her roasted potatoes with thyme and enough butter to melt anyone and even bring a smile to Scarborough's lips with each bite. It was nice getting to see some of the constant rigidity slip away, even for a little while. Scarborough often looked as though he expected the entire world to come gunning for him. And maybe it had. If his folks had fought all the time, then maybe he'd felt like he was in the center of the firing range. I didn't know, and it wasn't a good idea for me to speculate.

"How are things going, other than the new horse?" Dad asked Scarborough.

"Good," he answered between bites. "This is amazing." He ate his piece of the roast, and Mom filled his plate once more. "I wish we'd get some rain. That would always help."

"Yeah, it does. We either get deluged to the point where we have nothing but mud, or we get nothing and the ground is as dry as the Sahara. We're all lucky because we have a water source, but I'm afraid that after the winter we had, if we don't get some rain soon enough, that's going to start to run dry on us."

"I'm careful about what I pump and only use it for the animals and to run the house. I don't try to irrigate anything," Scarborough explained.

"None of us do, but that still means that pretty soon, there isn't going to be anything," I added. Every day I looked up at the sky in the mornings, praying for some clouds on the horizon, some sign that there was moisture heading our way. We needed it bad.

"We've weathered dry years before, and we'll do it again," Dad pronounced. It was part of the western water cycle, but all

23

of us around the table knew it was getting hotter and dryer, or it seemed that way.

"Maybe the end of the week. That's what they said on the radio." Scarborough finished eating his second helping about the time I finished my first. "Though if the weatherman could get things right, then we could actually plan our days based on them, at least once in a while."

"Tell me about it." Dad humphed, and since I was finished, I began clearing the table. Mom would certainly do it, but since she'd cooked, I wanted to help. Sometimes Mom seemed to have boundless energy, and at other times, she seemed tired. I supposed that was just part of getting older. At least that was all I hoped it was.

"You all go into the living room," Mom said about the time I had cleared away the last of the dishes. "I'll finish cleaning up, and I baked a cake this afternoon." She pushed back her chair and thanked me with a pat on the cheek.

"I need to check on some things in the barn," Dad said, excusing himself as well.

"Do you need help?" both Scarborough and I asked at the same time.

"No. You boys sit a little. I won't be long." Dad went out the front door, and Scarborough and I found ourselves alone in my parents' living room.

"So, what else is new?" I asked him. It seemed lame, but it wasn't like Scarborough was a conversation starter.

"Well…." He seemed to search. "Yeah… I got a letter a couple days ago. My high school class is having a twentieth class reunion back in Nebraska. They sent me an invitation. It's in a few weeks." He paused and sighed. "My dad went to a boarding school, and I used to hope he'd send me to get away from him, but he was too cheap." He scowled. "I don't think I'm going to go. It will be just a bunch of people I haven't seen in years sitting around and talking about all the good things that they've done and…." He settled back in the chair, and for a second, I wondered if he wanted the thing to swallow him up.

"Why not go?" I asked. "You haven't seen any of those people in a long time, right? Did you have friends back then?"

Scarborough pursed his lips. "I did. I haven't talked to any of them in a long time." A cloud passed over his features.

"Then go."

Scarborough nodded slowly. "It's a long drive and all." He scratched his head. "I thought about flying, but then I have to drive to Casper and fly halfway around the country so I can get to Omaha and then drive two hours from there. And that is if the planes actually take off. They get canceled a lot of the time because of weather and stuff."

"It just seems like a shame not to go and see some of your old friends," I said. "I can watch your place. You know that, and it isn't like you'd be gone for weeks."

The screen door banged closed behind Dad, and he shut the inner one. "There's lightning in the distance. I hope to hell it rains and this isn't a dry storm, or we'll be dealing with fires all over the place." He sat down, and the conversation changed back to the weather.

Thunder ticked the edge of what I could hear and then grew louder. I stood and went out onto the porch, with Scarborough following me. "I love the smell of a storm on the air." I wasn't sure how much actual moisture there was, but the thunder grew louder and then the wind shifted, becoming fierce and insistent, blowing the trees near the house hard.

"Dad, is the barn closed tight?" I asked, putting my head inside. I thought of my own and remembered that I had closed up everything before I came over.

"It's all set," he said, and I rejoined Scarborough on the porch. The wind had lessened and the moisture on the wind had increased.

"We should go inside," I said as the wind picked up again, this time carrying the rain. I pulled open the front door, and we got inside as the storm pummeled the side and front of the house, almost sounding like fists beating at the windows.

"This isn't going to last long," Dad said, looking at his phone. "The cell just popped up and it will move on fast."

The rain continued and then stopped just as quickly as it started. The good thing was that it was night, so the sun wasn't going to dry everything until morning. But short deluges weren't what we needed, even though any rain was a godsend. What we truly needed was a more soaking rain over time, not a deluge that mostly ran off the parched land. Still, it was unexpected and better than no rain at all.

"Come on in for some dessert, and then you can all go and see that everything is okay," Mom said.

We sat in the living room, and she brought in plates. Mom's chocolate cake was to die for. It was simple and rich, and damned if Scarborough didn't hum over it more than once. I tried to ignore the little sound of delight, but it went right to the base of my spine, settling there like a tiny bolt of energy.

The storm had moved well off by the time we finished the cake, and Scarborough stood, saying his good-nights. It was only nine, but all of us got up with the sun, so an early evening was expected.

Mom gave Scarborough another hug, which I think surprised him. "You need to come visit more often." She smiled and carried the dishes into the kitchen. Dad shook Scarborough's hand and then went to help her while I walked Scarborough out to his truck, knowing I needed to leave as well.

"You should go back to see your friends." Scarborough always seemed so alone. Maybe he liked it that way, but something about it bothered me in the pit of my belly.

"It's a long drive, and…."

"Then we could go together if you wanted," I found myself offering before I could actually believe what was coming out of my mouth. The two of us had largely an outdoor friendship, and now I was offering to go on a road trip with him to visit where he grew up. Granted, maybe a visit to his past was what Scarborough needed. Or maybe not, but he seemed unsure, and maybe what Scarborough needed was a friend. Lord, I didn't know, and part of me wished I could drag the words back into my mouth. Either way, the offer was made and I wasn't going to take it back. I did have my pride, after all.

Scarborough scrunched his face. "You want to go all the way to Nebraska? With me? You know my family isn't… well, I don't have to see them. But I would like to see some of my old friends. A lot of them have kids now and big families." He got a faraway look that I couldn't read. This was a whole new side to Scarborough that I had never seen before, and it made me curious as to the things about my friend that I had no idea about. "Are you really sure? It's in ten days, and I'm going to need to leave in a week if I'm going to go. It will take a few days to get there and all. The drive is boring as hell, that I can guarantee you, and you already know I'm shit for company."

I smiled. "Now you're trying to talk me out of it." He was cute sometimes, and I found myself staring into his intense blue eyes with flecks of purple. And what surprised me was how he didn't look away. Maybe I had been right and this was what Scarborough needed.

Sex and what Scarborough did for it, if anything, was something he and I had never talked about. I knew he was gay just because I got that vibe from him, and because of a few comments he had made over the years. Mom knew he was gay too—otherwise she wouldn't have decided to try to fix the two of us up—but any details of his love life were almost as big a mystery as so much else about the man. Still, the way he looked at me, with his lips parted slightly and his eyes as wide as the huge blue hydrangeas that Mom grew on the north side of the house…. My throat went dry, and for a few seconds, my mind raced forward with ideas about Scarborough that I knew were completely stupid. He had never shown any particular interest in me that way, in all the years I'd known him, so why would that change now?

"Not really. I just want you to know what the deal is." He pulled open the door to his truck. "I'll see you when you come to work with the horse, and I can make arrangements to go to Nebraska." He got in the truck and drove away as I stared after him, wondering what the hell I had just gotten myself into.

CHAPTER 3

"How is it going?" Scarborough asked as he slowly approached the paddock. He leaned on the railing and thankfully made no fast movements. "I've decided to call him Storm."

"Good name, isn't it?" I said softly to the horse, his ears flicking forward to pick up what I was saying. Storm was surprisingly responsive and had at one time been trained, to a degree, which made my job easier. What I needed to do was to try to tap into the earlier training without triggering whatever trauma had sent this beautiful boy over the edge.

After a week, I'd managed to get a long lead on his halter and slowly lead him around the paddock. I could tell that the wildness lay just below the surface and that Storm was ready to break loose at any second. The longer I worked with him and just let him walk with me, the more some of the tension left him after a while.

After an hour working with him, I released him from the lead. Storm hurried away like a kid who had been cooped inside all day and was finally granted recess.

"What do you think?"

I shrugged. "It's like every time he does something, Storm is afraid of getting hit. I'd love to know who owned him before so I can go on over there and kick the living shit out of them. It will take some time, but I think he'll settle down. Though I'll hazard a guess that he will never be ridden by anyone again. There's no trust left in him. He'd bolt for no reason and that would be that.

Any rider, no matter how experienced, would never be able to trust him at all."

"I see. But he will be good for stud?" Scarborough asked.

"Yes. If you can get some information on his breeding—and that is going to take some doing. Whoever sold him probably changed his name, and I bet he isn't registered anywhere. He has a huge number of amazing characteristics that mean he should have incredible offspring. I would think that you could do very well with him, but he isn't going to be of any other use." Still, I thought I could get him to the point where he wouldn't be so spooked all the time, and maybe he could be more easily managed than he was today.

"I got some reservations for the trip, and I thought that we could leave tomorrow. The reunion people know that I'm coming with a guest, and…." He seemed a little fidgety, but if I had been honest, I was interested in seeing where Scarborough came from and learning more about him.

"I'll be ready to go. I wanted to work with him again before we left. He and I are finally making some progress. Dad said he was going to watch our places while we're gone."

Scarborough nodded. "There isn't much to do for the week, but when I get back, there will be a lot, especially if we get some more rain." The fields had greened up again after another evening shower, and it seemed they could get another cutting of hay to put into the barns. "I have things out for your dad so he won't have to look for stuff. I tried to make it easier for him."

Tension rolled off Scarborough, and I wondered if there was something I could say to ease it. But honestly, it was none of my business. I didn't understand why he felt that way other than maybe not wanting to rely on anyone for anything.

"I need to run into town to get a few things before we leave," I offered, changing the subject. Beau, who had been sitting near the side of the corral as I worked with Storm, hurried over as soon as I mentioned going somewhere. He knew I was leaving and for the last few days had stuck to me like glue. "You know you have to stay with Dad on this trip." He'd be fine and would have my dad's dogs to play with. Still, I felt bad leaving him behind. "Do you need anything in town?"

Scarborough nodded.

"Then let's go together and save a trip."

We piled into my truck, with the windows lowered, the air rushing around us as we headed to town. The heat of the last few days had abated, but it would be back, that was certain. It was nice to have the windows down and some fresh air for a change. Beau loved it, his nose pointed to the breeze as he sat in his place in the cramped back seat.

Town was small, with a single main street. Still, it had everything we needed. Someone had been foresighted years ago and put the businesses back a little from the sidewalk and planted trees that lined the street, providing some much-needed shade. I was lucky enough to find a parking spot and pulled right into the shady place, then turned off the engine. "Beau, you need to stay." We got out, and I left the windows down for air. Beau was well trained and I knew he'd stay inside.

"Hardware store?" I asked, and Scarborough nodded, so we headed that way. I waved to a few people as they crossed the street ahead of us, hurrying to the far side. At first I wondered if something was going on, but it became clear pretty quickly that our side of the street had emptied and all the foot traffic was on the other one. I ignored it and continued on as though nothing was happening, and pulled open the door to the hardware store.

"Clyde," I said with a smile at the man who had owned the store for as long as I could remember. "How are you doing?" He was seventy-five if he was a day.

"My legs," he said quietly. Clyde had been hurt as a child in an accident. "The kids say I should quit working and take it easy." He looked around. "Albert wants to get his hands on this place and turn it into his version of Home Depot or something." He huffed, and Scarborough wandered off, probably to get what he needed. Clyde watched him as though he were some sort of curiosity, but didn't say anything. "What do you need?"

"Scarborough and I are heading to Nebraska for a little while, and I need some oats. I want to make sure Dad doesn't run out while I'm gone, since he and his guys will be taking care of things for me. They're watching over Scarborough's place too."

Clyde's eyes narrowed for a second. "Your mom and dad are good folks." His gaze shifted to Scarborough, who carried some tools and an off-brand toaster to the counter.

"You need feed or anything?" I asked, and Scarborough shook his head as Clyde rang him up. Scarborough paid in cash and waited while Clyde bagged his purchases without either of them saying a word.

"I'll wait out in the truck." Scarborough took the bag, muttered a thank-you to Clyde, and left the store.

"What is all this about?" I asked. "People crossing the street and shit?" I met his gaze, daring him not to tell me.

Clyde relaxed slightly. "Just rumors, I guess. People talking about other people the way they do." He sighed. "Should know by now not to listen to the busybodies in town. Got more talk in 'em than sense." He seemed more like himself. "Is he doing okay? The man spends too much time alone. Folks start flapping their gums, making shit up, I suppose."

He rang up what I needed and told me the damage. I paid and said I'd load the feed myself. I waved goodbye and went around the side, threw two bags of feed over my shoulders, and carried them to the truck to put them in back. I got two more and then pulled open the driver's door.

Living in a small town meant that everyone helped one another and everyone knew everyone's business. Which meant that everyone was up in your business sometimes too. Not much happened in a place like Red Rock, so sometimes folks got to talking and started thinking of ways to make things happen. I swear there were times when folks flapping their lips made more breeze than the wind.

"You need anything else?" I asked Scarborough. "Maybe a shake or something?"

"Nothing for me. I need to get back to the ranch so I can be ready to go tomorrow." He turned to pat Beau's head lightly, so I started the engine and pulled out of the parking spot. "I know what people are saying. I hear stuff sometimes." He chuckled, but without mirth. "Apparently sometimes I have two heads or a third eye or something." He was making light of it, but I knew it got to him.

"Okay…," I said. "People talk all the damned time. Too much, if you ask me." Suddenly I was not at all interested in what sort of exaggerations the people in Red Rock had come up with. These were supposed to be decent, good, go-to-church-on-Sunday people.

Scarborough shrugged. "Doesn't really matter," he said, and continued stroking Beau's head and back as we left town proper behind, heading toward home.

I dropped Scarborough at his place and then went on to mine, got caught up on my chores, and put all my purchases away. Dad knew where I kept my supplies for the horses. I brought down enough hay for the week and parceled out the sweet feed as well. Then I cleaned all the stalls and laid fresh bedding. Beau, of course, kept me company the way he usually did.

"Is there anything special I need to watch out for?" Dad asked, and I nearly dropped my shovel. I hadn't heard him approach.

"Not that I know of. Everything is ready, and I have a stall that you can put your horse in when you get it." I showed him the one I had ready.

Dad nodded. "Are you sure this is a good idea? You going with him?"

I set the shovel aside and rubbed my chin with a gloved hand. "A week ago, you and Mom were pushing the two of us together, and now you ask a question like that. What gives? Is this whatever was buzzing in town? People were rude as shit, Dad." I pulled off my gloves to let my sweaty hands dry off and breathe.

"I know. I heard. And yeah, it was a stupid question." He pulled back and grew quiet once again, wandering away and taking a look at things.

I put on my gloves again so I could finish up. "People talk all the damned time," I added.

Dad nodded. He had obviously decided there had been enough talk, because he simply wandered through the barn and then outside. I finished up my chores, put the tools away, and found Dad sitting on my porch, his phone in hand, sending messages.

"You want a beer?" I asked, and he seemed to assent. I got a couple and returned, and Beau sat next to my chair. We drank and didn't say anything, which was fine. There was nothing to be said. I was sure whatever was circulating about Scarborough was just rumor and idle minds. They would move on to something else soon enough. If you gave gossip any credence, then it tended to hang around.

Dad set his phone aside and finished his beer. "Have a good trip tomorrow." Dad put the beer bottle on the table, stood, and ambled out to his truck.

I waited until he was gone, then wandered inside to take a shower and make a quick dinner. More than once, in the quiet hours of the evening, I wondered what it was going to be like spending hours alone in the truck with Scarborough. Not that it mattered. He and I were destined to be friends, just friends. And the idea that my mother had planted about anything more, well… that idea needed to die as quickly as it had sprouted.

The trouble was, just about the time I thought I had killed off the idea, it sprang to life again as soon as I saw Scarborough. He didn't give me any indication that he felt the same way. It was all in my head and my dick, and I needed to let it go.

CHAPTER 4

BEAU WAS pissed the following morning when I took him to Mom and Dad's. He looked at me as though I were a traitor, and when I drove away, the howl from inside the house was nearly too much to bear. I almost called Scarborough to tell him I was going to bring Beau along, but that wouldn't have been fair to Beau. He didn't need to be cooped up in the truck for hours on end.

I returned to the house, did one more walk-through, and then had my bag ready on the porch.

Once Scarborough pulled in, I put my things in the back seat and we were off. Shania Twain sang from the speakers, and for a few seconds, I actually thought I might have seen Scarborough smile.

"Are you excited about this reunion?"

"Maybe a little."

"What about your dad? Does he know you're coming?" I asked, thinking it would be a shame if he didn't at least try to see him. No one could change someone else's mind when they were set in their ways.

"He knows. My sister told him. I have no idea if he'll see me at all, but he knows where I'll be. Now the rest is up to him."

That cloud I'd seen before passed over his features, and I knew in my heart that no matter what he said, it hurt him a lot. That pissed me off something fierce, though I had no right to be. It was Scarborough's business, not mine…. Still it made me mad for him.

"Then it's his loss if he doesn't come see you." That was the truth, as far as I was concerned.

Scarborough gripped the wheel tighter as he got on the road, heading south toward the main freeway system. "That's nice to say, but he won't see it that way." He turned up the music, and I sat back. There was nothing I could do, so I watched the rolling hills out the window as they slipped by.

Hour after hour, mile after mile, passed under the tires, and we finally reached the freeway and were able to go faster.

"You know," I finally said, after I realized it was nearing noon and he and I had said maybe three words to each other in the last three hours, most of which were about trying to find a bathroom, "sometimes silence is golden, and other times it's a pain in the ass."

Scarborough turned to look at me. "I never was very good at small talk."

"Bullshit. Lord save me from silent and broody cowboys. That's my dad all over, and half the time when I was a kid, I thought he was mad at me because he didn't say shit about crap. So talk. Tell me what it was like growing up in Nebraska. I've known you for a long time, and yet I feel like I don't know all that much about you."

Scarborough shrugged. "Ain't much for me to tell. I grew up like lots of kids thereabouts. Mom and Dad went to church on Sunday, and they carried it with them wherever they went. My mom used to scold us when we were bad by saying that we were making baby Jesus cry. You know the routine, I'm sure."

Now it was my turn to shrug. "You've met my parents. They went to church, but they lived practical lives, and Dad was a cafeteria kind of man. He picked and chose what he wanted to believe in." I loved the fact that Scarborough smiled. "Dad didn't talk much, but when I asked him once, he told me he felt closest to God when he was outside."

Scarborough's attention returned fully to the road. "Not my people. Anyway, I worked and went to school. When I got home, there was always a list of chores. We worked hard, and we worked a lot."

That didn't surprise me. Mom and Dad did the same. I had my chores to do, but I got paid for doing them. Mom felt it important that work should be rewarded.

"Did you get an allowance?"

Scarborough shook his head. "Mom and Dad called it food. If I wanted money for something, I had to go out and earn it somewhere else. So I worked on other folks' farms too. My life from the time I was about nine was work and more work. And it was funny, because when I did have money, Mom and Dad suddenly found ways that I had to spend it. Like if I worked half the summer to buy a bicycle because the other kids had one, suddenly I needed clothes for school and the money would be gone. But Mom and Dad bought my sisters' clothes for school."

I realized two things in that moment. Scarborough carried a huge amount of resentment, and we were going about a hundred miles an hour.

He slowed down and took a deep breath.

"I'm sorry. I had things I had to buy too, but they told me what they were ahead of time. And Mom always saw to it that I had some money in my pocket. She was real good that way." I paused, figuring I'd change the subject. "Did you do 4-H or FFA?"

"4-H," he answered. "One year I raised a steer. I bought it with my own money and told Dad I wanted to raise it for the fair. He said he didn't have room in the barn for it. Our neighbor, Mr. Thompson, let me have room in his barn, and I went over and fed and watered it every day for almost a year. He was a beauty and grew huge." Scarborough smiled once again. "He won in his division that year and came in second overall."

"Doesn't the livestock go to auction?"

Scarborough nodded. "He sold for a huge price, and they made the check out to me. Dad told me I should give it to him, but I remember shaking my head and putting it in my pocket. The next day I went down to a different bank than the one Mom and Dad used and opened an account. I put the money there. They were pissed, but that evening Mr. Thompson came over and told me how proud he was of me, and that since I had done all the work, whatever I got was well earned. After that, they didn't say anything more about it."

"Shit...," I swore softly. "You shouldn't have to have the neighbor come to your rescue just to keep what you worked for." What was the point of working hard if there wasn't some sort of reward? That seemed so stupid to me.

"After I graduated high school, I left as soon as I could get the hell out of town."

"Is that why your dad won't talk to you? He's pissed you left."

"No. I worked for a ranch outside town and stayed there in the bunkhouse. One of the other hands was older, and he was nice to me... and he liked me... that way. The owners were nice and open-minded. They were concerned that he might be taking advantage, but once word got back to my folks, that was it." Scarborough sat straighter in the seat. "After that, I decided I wasn't going to be beholden or rely on anyone else for anything. If my mom and dad didn't give a crap about me when they knew who I was, why would anyone else?"

It felt like someone had knocked the wind out of me. "You know not everyone is like that. People will like you for who you are if you let them see you. Mom and Dad like you, and you're my friend... and I see you." Well, at least maybe I was seeing part of him for the very first time, but I wasn't going to kick Scarborough out for something like that.

He shook his head. "Ain't nobody that really sees me. Not those people in town who make up stories and shit."

I knew how he felt. "But maybe you have to *let* people see you." I swallowed, wondering just what he and I were walking into in Nebraska. "Did you leave a lot of friends behind when you left?"

"I think so. My class wasn't very big in school, but I played basketball in the winter and I was pretty good at it. Never going to be anything other than some fun and some time away from the farm, but Dad was proud that I was good at something. So I got to play. But only in the winter when there weren't as many chores and stuff." Scarborough smiled once again. "I'm looking forward to seeing some of my teammates again. Maybe we can get up a game. Did you play?"

"I was generally into sports and things, but I wasn't good at basketball. Just a little too short. I liked baseball, though, and I played football when I was young. Mom put an end to that when I got hit when I was twelve and the doctor thought I might have a concussion. I remember it was one of the few arguments Mom and Dad had, and she put her foot down. Mom can be tough when she needs to be, and she wasn't going to have me getting hurt like that. Dad still wanted me to play, and finally they just asked me what I wanted. I said I'd rather ride and do junior rodeo. Not that Mom was any more thrilled, but they let me make the decision." I supposed that was one of the big differences between Scarborough's family and mine. Mom especially let me make decisions. I know Dad would have made them all if she had let him, but in the end, they asked me what I wanted. I suspected no one had ever asked Scarborough much of anything.

Scarborough slowed down, the sky darkening as we approached I-80 late in the afternoon. He made the turn onto the freeway and continued heading east.

"Some sort of storm is blowing up," I told him, and Scarborough nodded but continued moving.

"I hope we'll drive out of it," he said, but either it was moving faster than we were or the storm was growing around us. Either way, the sky continued to darken. "Watch out for twisters. It's that time of year, and this kind of storm could produce one." Scarborough gripped the wheel so tightly, his knuckles turned white. I craned my neck to peer out every window just to see if there was something coming up on us.

The rain sounded like bullets against the truck and instantly poured over the roof and down the windows. There was no shelter of any kind ahead, and even with the wipers on fast, there was no seeing anything at all. Scarborough pulled off to the side and put on his hazard lights, and we sat in the middle of a torrent as other cars and trucks plodded on past. Someone pulled up behind us, and we sat, looking out the windows, waiting for the rain to pass. "These sorts of things blow up this time of year, and then they're gone."

"I can't see anything."

"It's raining. The twister is usually toward the leading edge, if there is one. We should be okay if we just wait out the rain."

As if on cue, the sky lightened and the rain let up. Scarborough pulled back out onto the road and continued forward. We didn't go particularly fast. Even so, Scarborough jammed on the brakes as a shape loomed out of the humidity and fog ahead of us. I braced myself, hoping we didn't add to the accident, heart pounding in my ears as Scarborough skidded to a stop along the shoulder. A truck lay on its side across a lane and a half of the freeway. Other cars had pulled off to the side, and a group of people were out directing traffic. It looked like others had one of the cab doors open and were getting the driver out.

"Jesus," I said softly.

"The winds can come with a lot of force here." Scarborough continued forward slowly until we got past the truck and then gradually picked up speed as the skies continued to lighten and visibility improved.

"I think I need to change my shorts," I joked, and Scarborough actually laughed. It was a surprisingly happy, tension-free sound, and just what we needed.

"We get storms at home, but usually not like these. With the land so flat, there's nothing to stop them building, and the wind will blow in a straight line with nothing in its way," Scarborough explained. "Mom lived in fear of the weather," he continued, and I remained quiet, letting him talk. It was pretty cool, getting to know him. We had spent just part of a day together, and I sort of felt a little closer to him. It was nice. Of course, after that adrenaline spike, his scent, spicy and warm, intensified, and I had to do my best to keep myself from looking over at him every few minutes.

"When we were kids, she could smell rain on the air, and then she'd start hunkering down. I was fourteen and working in the barn to get it cleaned up when she raced out, grabbed me by the arm, and tugged me out and into the storm cellar. The house had no basement, but there was also a shelter near the barn. Dad was somewhere else, but I remember hearing the deep, almost humming wind noise. People say a twister sounds like a freight train, but I heard one that day, and it sounds like nothing else I have ever heard—so much wind, a howl in the air that makes your ears want to pop out of your head. The damned thing went right overhead and only grew more and more intense before passing by."

"Good God."

"It wasn't like *The Wizard of Oz* at all, I can tell you that. The twister passed over the house and touched down just east of the farm. It took out the neighbor's house and barn, leveled the entire farm with just matchsticks left, but ours was fine." When he turned toward me, his eyes had this wild look, like he wasn't just remembering but reliving that event. Maybe he was.

I gently placed my hand on his shoulder. "I love watching storms sometimes."

"I hate them. They remind me that there's nothing you can do about them and that suddenly everything you have and built can be taken away in seconds."

Thankfully the clouds cleared and the sun came out once again, but Scarborough's mood took longer to shift.

"Where's the hotel?"

"Almost an hour up the freeway," Scarborough answered. I was a little worried about the kind of place he'd chosen. I knew it wasn't going to be fancy, but when we finally pulled off the freeway, there was the sign for a bargain hotel that looked as though it had been built at the same time as the original Route 66 and hadn't been updated since. Taking a deep breath, I determined that I wasn't going to say anything and would make the best of it. Scarborough didn't say anything either as we pulled in.

"Stay here a minute," he said, and got out of the truck.

I catalogued in my mind the various diseases and fungi that I was going to find growing in the bathroom. I wasn't a neat freak or anything, but after living with my mother, who never met a stain she didn't attack as though she were going to war, I was used to a clean home. I kept my own nearly as clean as Mom kept hers, and….

My thoughts skidded to a halt as Scarborough got in, closed the door, and backed out of the lot. He returned to the highway and got off at the next exit. I breathed a sigh of relief at the Holiday Inn Express we pulled into.

"I hope this is nice. I haven't stayed at a hotel… well… I never did before."

I stared at him, wide-eyed. "You never went anywhere as a kid?"

Scarborough scoffed. "Are you kidding? Did my parents sound like the kind of ones to take us all on a wonderful family vacation? We never went anywhere. One time, we were supposed to go to a family wedding in Omaha, but Mom wasn't feeling well, so we stayed home." He picked a parking spot and stopped. "Once

I left home, I couldn't afford a hotel. I slept in my truck until I was able to find my first job. And even then, sometimes I still did if they didn't have a place for me." He got out, and I grabbed the bags and followed Scarborough inside.

I thought he might have been pulling my leg about the whole hotel thing, but the way he looked around as soon as he stepped inside told me a lot. The lobby wasn't huge, but it was tall, and Scarborough looked at it like it was the Ritz. I kept wondering how anyone could go through life and not have stayed in a hotel, but when you didn't have anything, a truck was as good a shelter as any, and it beat sleeping out in the rain.

"Can I help you?"

"Yes, ma'am. I called ahead for a room at this hotel." He smiled and took off his hat. I did the same and let Scarborough go through the check-in process. "I don't have a credit card. I can pay cash. We won't be making any phone calls or nothing." Scarborough pulled out his wallet and paid for the room with twenties. She gave him the key cards, and I smiled as Scarborough took them.

"You room is on the third floor, and the elevator is right down that hall."

I hefted the luggage and followed Scarborough, and we rode up to the third floor and went down the hallway to our room. I took one of the key cards and put it in the lock before opening the door.

"How does that not unlock all the rooms?"

"There's a code on the magnetic strip that tells the lock that this is our room. It won't work anywhere else." I went inside and waited for Scarborough. There were two beds, and I let him choose the one he wanted while I turned on the air-conditioning to start cooling the room.

"Do we need that?"

"Yes," I said softly.

"Don't we have to pay for it?" Scarborough asked, and I shook my head.

"Air-conditioning comes with the room, so we can sleep with it nice and cool. Go ahead and check out the bathroom if you want. I'm going to see what sort of food is nearby, and we can eat." I was getting hungry and figured I'd take us out for dinner.

"This is nice," Scarborough said. "I wasn't sure if this was an expensive hotel or not. But I wanted to find a place kind of nice for us to stay. That hotel out by the highway smelled funny." He crinkled his nose. "Not that I was going to stay there." He came out and sat on the edge of the bed, sort of staring at the walls. "What do we do now?"

"There's a restaurant next door, and we can eat there. The town is another mile away or so, but we can watch television or go into town. Whichever you feel like." We had been in the truck all day, and I was just grateful not to be moving for a while.

"I guess I'm hungry." He seemed nervous, probably about the reunion and being back.

We left the hotel and went next door. The hostess gave us a table right away. The place was one of those diner-type chain restaurants. The food was cheap and okay. Apparently Scarborough liked it, because he ate every bite of his hamburger, as well as the fries and his salad.

"This is better than my own cooking at home."

"What do you make for yourself?" I asked as I ate the last of my salad.

"Sandwiches mostly, especially when I'm in a hurry. But I cook some, especially when the garden is coming in. I also grill out sometimes. Generally easy stuff—nothing like what your mom makes."

I pushed what was left of my plate away. "Nobody cooks like my mom. I don't think it's humanly possible." But Scarborough seemed happy enough.

"Aren't you going to eat?" He pointed to my plate.

I shrugged. "The burger was dry, and…."

The server had just appeared and took the plate. "Then let me get you something else," she said, and gave me a menu, so I ordered some chicken.

That tasted better, and when the check came, neither of my dishes was on it. I paid the bill, leaving a nice tip, and we walked back to the hotel, the evening warm but with a nice breeze on the air. The air movement was just enough to be refreshing and keep the humidity at bay.

"Thank you for dinner," Scarborough said as he looked upward. "It seems strange for it to be light and me not working."

"You know there is time for fun too." I smiled. "Come on. Let's get into that truck of yours. There's a town just down there, and we can see if there's anything to do." Scarborough seemed shocked. "We can sit in the room if you want." I waited while he unlocked the door, then climbed in and gave him directions.

It wasn't much more than a small farming community with a church, a small school that seemed to house all grades, a bar, a few businesses, and a feedstore. Basically, a farming support center near a rail line. The place looked tired, like it had been standing up to the heat and wind of the prairie for a long time. I looked at the bar, but it seemed just a watering hole. I was no stranger to those, but I wanted something fun to do, and that didn't seem like the thing.

I turned to the south, and flashing lights caught my eye. "What's going on over there?" I asked a lady as she passed on the sidewalk.

"The carnival? The Rotary club puts it on to raise money for the town." She smiled and continued on her way.

"Come on. Let's go!" I was already heading that way. When I turned, Scarborough looked at me like I'd gone nuts. "I know, you've never been to one. But I think it's about time. There will be rides, games, and enough junk food to give you a bellyache." I pointed, and we walked on over.

"You're really serious about this?" Scarborough asked. "This is for kids."

"It's for everybody. And maybe it's time you let yourself be a kid for just a little while." I patted his arm. At the entrance to the carnival, I bought tickets and headed for the Ferris wheel, which we got in line for.

"How tall is that thing?" Scarborough asked, looking upward.

"It's fine. There's air up there." I handed the attendant the tickets for both of us, and we got into the gondola. It swayed, and Scarborough clutched the bar in front. He gasped as we began moving and then stopped, rocking back and forth.

"I don't think I like this," he whispered.

"Why not? Look over there. Your truck is down there, and the town is right over where those lights are." I pointed, and he finally let go of the rail with one hand. "It's okay," I added as we moved again, then stopped at the very top. Afterward, we went down, the ride continuing without stopping for a while. I took Scarborough's hand and squeezed his fingers lightly. "Remember, this is supposed to be fun."

Scarborough laughed and sat back instead of acting like he was ready to jump out as soon as we got close to the ground. "I remember when carnivals came to town as part of the fair. I never got to go. Dad said that they were a waste of money and that the games were just to cheat people."

I huffed. "I can't imagine a fair in town and you actually were there because you had animals entered but couldn't go on anything. That's just cruel." The ride came to an end, and we got off. "What do you want to do next?" I pressed the tickets into his hand, and we headed over to a ride that went around fast and tilted on its side. I was shocked, but it seemed that once I'd broken the ice, Scarborough wanted to do everything. We went on ride after ride, until we were out of tickets.

"Can we play games?"

"Sure," I said with a smile. "Though they are designed so you lose. You have to know that." I grinned, figuring what the hell. He was having a good time and smiling. There was nothing I was going to do to change that.

"There's a shooting range," Scarborough said, hurrying in that direction. He paid the five dollars and sighted the gun. "I have to shoot the entire star away?"

"Yes," the attendant said.

I wanted to warn him that it was a setup, but Scarborough started shooting. By the time his gun was empty, the paper was shredded, and when he pulled it back, the star was indeed gone. Scarborough collected his prize, a huge stuffed animal, and handed it to me.

"Can I do it again?" Scarborough asked.

"We aren't going to have room in the truck," I told him, but the attendant took another five, and in the end, we each ended up walking through the carnival with a huge dog under our arms until we filled the back seat with them and headed to the hotel.

"That was fun."

"Where did you learn to shoot like that? Those guns are usually wonky."

"Oh, it was. The thing pulled to the left, but once I got it figured out, all I had to do was shoot in a large circle and the star just fell away. It was that simple." He grinned. "I did a lot of hunting growing up. It was part of how we fed the family. Dad made sure I knew how to shoot almost before I could walk." A cloud passed over Scarborough's features.

"Let's head back to the hotel. We have to get up early and have a ways to drive yet." Nebraska was a long state. Thank goodness the speed limit was seventy-five and we could move. Once we reached the hotel, Scarborough went inside, but I walked across the street to the gas station and bought some snacks for the road, then carried them back into the room.

I opened the door and must have taken Scarborough by surprise, because he was standing by the end of his bed, naked, stepping into his shorts. Damn, the man was stunning, and I closed the door quickly and forgot that I wasn't supposed to be staring, but it was too damned tempting not to look. "What happened to you?" I asked without thinking. Fine lines crisscrossed Scarborough's back.

He grabbed the T-shirt off the bed and pulled it on right away before turning back to me. "When Dad found me after high school with another boy, he decided to try to beat the sin out of me. He got in a few good hits with the strap. The one thing he wasn't counting on was me fighting back. I stood up to him and yanked the belt away from him. It was then that I realized I couldn't stay there anymore."

"Your father did that to you?" I sat next to him, trying not to look at his bare legs with their dusting of brown. "Dad and I didn't always see eye to eye on everything, but he never did that sort of thing to me." I wanted to take his hand and provide some sort of comfort, but what in the hell did one do to soothe away that kind of hurt? "No wonder you never went back. I mean, I know that people aren't always accepting, but to have your dad treat you that way…." I leaned closer to him and then on impulse kissed his shoulder before standing and going to my own bed.

I couldn't look at Scarborough for a while. He seemed so raw at the moment, and damn it all, if I had turned toward him, he'd see exactly what he did to me, and that would be embarrassing. Scarborough was my friend, and I needed to remember that. The idea that my mom had put in my head—the damned thing having decided to grow—needed to die instead… and fast. "I'm going to go get a shower." Maybe I could have a few minutes of privacy to take care of what I needed to before I made a complete fool of myself.

"Martin," he said softly, and I hazarded a glance his way. "You know I don't talk about stuff… so why did I tell you?" He didn't move, and I grabbed my clothes to carry to the bathroom. "I don't understand it."

"I'm your friend, and you spend most of your life alone. Maybe it's natural for you to want to talk about things sometimes. Most people do." I wanted to hide in the bathroom, get cleaned up, and go to bed so my head would stop with the images of Scarborough that ran through my mind.

"I guess so." Scarborough slid back on the bed on top of the covers. He turned on the television and began flipping through the channels.

I went to the bathroom and closed the door, relieved for a few minutes to myself. I tugged off my shirt and the rest of my clothes, then started the water. It took a second to warm, and then I got in, washing away the sweat and dirt from the road. Sometimes there was nothing better than getting clean, and it sure as hell felt amazingly good.

I tried not to think about Scarborough just outside the door, and washed up, running my soapy fingers through my hair before rinsing everything away. I thought about giving myself some relief, but then I heard Scarborough moving through the room outside, and every damned time I closed my eyes, I pictured him in front of me. In the end, I turned off the water, dried off, and put on some nightclothes. Grabbing the dirty things, I carried them out into the dark room with me.

Scarborough had the covers pulled tight around him, the television off, the air conditioner humming softly. I got into bed and rolled over, trying not to listen to Scarborough's breathing. He didn't seem to snore, but instead made these gentle sounds that I could barely hear over the fan. Scarborough rolled over, and in the darkness, I could just make out his form in the bed.

I wondered what it would be like to crawl into the other bed and press up against him, hold him, maybe even run my hands over the scars on his back just to show him that they didn't bother me. Hell, I wanted to get to know every inch of him, from those white lines to the way his chest and belly felt under my hands. I wanted to know what he tasted like and how he kissed. Was he the kind of guy who let others take charge, or did he give as good as he got? I just wanted to know.

I rolled over once again, facing away from him to try to get my head to stop running through question after question. We had to be up early in the morning and get on the road so we could get there in time to check in to the next hotel and change our clothes for the first gathering of the reunion. Somehow I needed to get this head of mine to calm down so I could get to sleep.

Eventually, I managed to close my eyes and fall to sleep, but only after tossing for a while.

CHAPTER 5

IN THE early afternoon, Scarborough and I drove into the town where he grew up. It was slightly bigger than where we had stayed the night before, with a sign over the main street welcoming the graduating class of 1999 to their twenty-year reunion. Throughout the morning, Scarborough had become more nervous, and as we passed under the sign, he pulled into a parking spot and just sat there.

"Maybe this was a bad idea. I should have stayed home. They always say you can't go back, and when I think about it, there's nothing for me here."

"How do you know? You said you had friends here." I tried to encourage him but had very little ammunition. The stories he'd told me about his family were dark enough that I had to wonder why he set foot in the state at all. "Concentrate on the people you want to see and let go of the rest if you can." What the hell else was I supposed to say? We were already here. "Let's go to the hotel. We can check in and get changed and cleaned up. You said some people were meeting for dinner at a brew pub. We can go there. It isn't likely your dad or anyone from your family is going to be there." I had never seen him like this. Not that I didn't think that Scarborough worried about things or got upset. It was just that he'd never let me see it before. Him being upset didn't bother me. I could handle whatever Scarborough might feel. But I really wanted him happy. He looked so wonderful when he smiled.

We sat there with the engine running, and then Scarborough lowered his window. "Buddy?" he asked, and a man stopped, then turned and hurried over.

"Scarry? Is that you?" He grinned. "I heard you were coming to the reunion, and I couldn't believe it. No one has heard anything about you in such a long time." He peered in the window. "Is this your boyfriend?" Apparently, word had gotten around about Scarborough. At least everyone in town didn't feel the same way his parents did.

"Martin is a good friend," Scarborough said. "He came with me so I wouldn't have to make the trip alone." He paused. "Do you still live here?"

Buddy shook his head. "No, my wife and I live in Seattle now. I met Gwen at college, and her family lives there. The kids are with their grandparents and having the time of their life, I'm sure." He straightened up and looked around. "This place looks the same, a little tired, but I guess it's home." He smiled and leaned into the open window. "Are you coming to the pub tonight?"

"That was the plan," I answered. Scarborough seemed a little overwhelmed.

"Wonderful. We'll see both of you there. I can't wait to find out what you've been up to." Buddy patted the door and stepped back. "I need to be off, but I'll see you later. Maybe we can get up a game tomorrow." He hurried down the street, and Scarborough raised the window. He pulled out of the parking spot and continued to the hotel. This was nothing like the one we stayed at last night. It wasn't a chain, but a small hotel at the edge of town that might have been a mansion of some type at one time.

"I hope it's okay. They made special arrangements for people from the reunion to stay here." He pulled into the small parking lot, and I got out and collected the bags from around the stuffed toys Scarborough had won.

The hotel was warm and inviting. Scarborough checked us in, and then we went up the stairs to the room in the back. "I hope it's okay to share a room."

I hadn't thought we'd do anything else.

Scarborough unlocked the door and went inside. I followed and stared at the king-size bed in the room.

"I asked for two beds, but they said they didn't have any other rooms. Maybe I should try to find another hotel or something." Scarborough sat on the edge of the bed, reaching for the phone.

"It's okay," I told him, setting down the bags and turning away. Damn, this was going to be quite interesting. I had shared a bed on many occasions, especially on the rodeo circuit. Saving money, especially on travel, was the name of the game. But I had never been attracted to someone the way Scarborough pulled at me, and I needed to get myself under control. It was only going to be for a few nights, and then we'd head back home. I could keep my hands to myself, and the bed *was* a king-size. There would be plenty of room. I turned on the air conditioner and stood in the flow of cool air. "Let's get unpacked and stuff. What time are you supposed to meet your friends?"

"Five thirty," Scarborough answered, without looking at me.

"Then we don't have very long," I said. "I really think this is going to be fun for you. Especially if the other guys are like Buddy." When he didn't move, I asked, "Do you mind if I clean up first?"

"Go ahead. I'll use the bathroom when you're done." Scarborough finally stood up, and I got the clothes I intended to wear and went to get ready. I showered quickly and didn't waste time, got dressed, and then left the bathroom for Scarborough. He scurried by me, barely lifting his gaze, and I wondered what had him so flustered. Sometimes I wished guys would just say what was on their mind rather than holding every fucking thing inside.

If I knew what was wrong, then I could try to fix it. But as it was, there was nothing I could do, so I finished getting ready.

Once I was dressed, I grabbed Scarborough's keys and went out to the truck, hauled in the stuffed dogs, and placed them on the bed. Scarborough laughed when he came out of the bathroom wearing only a towel. "I figured it would be best if we didn't have stuffed toys in the back of the truck the whole time we're in town." My throat went dry at all that skin, and I forgot what else I was going to say. Heat raced through me, and I tugged at my collar.

"Is something wrong?" Scarborough asked.

I shook my head. "Look, you know I'm gay, and so are you. And, well, maybe you don't know that you're some kind of wet dream walking around in only a towel." Jesus, I could hardly believe I was saying that.

Scarborough grabbed his clothes out of the suitcase. "I am not. I'm just some farm kid from Nebraska."

I shook my head and walked over to open the bathroom door. "Take a look. If all you are is a farm guy from Nebraska, then boy am I glad I came along, because if the guys here all look like you…." I couldn't help smiling.

Scarborough shrugged. "It doesn't matter what I look like on the outside. It's what I am and who I am on the inside, and I can't see anyone wanting to be with me." He picked up his clothes and returned to the bathroom, closing the door.

I sat on the edge of the bed, completely shocked. Good God, what else was there in Scarborough's past? I thought I understood some of why he was so careful with money. That made sense, and I could understand low self-esteem and not wanting to be hurt, since the people who should have looked out for him the most had done the most damage.

I had the feeling that Scarborough wasn't going to want to talk about things any further, so I turned on the television in order to take the pressure off. Hell, I was surprised Scarborough had told me all the things he had. I sent a message to Mom and let her know that we'd arrived safely and that we were going out to the reunion, which started tonight. She sent me a *Love you* message, and I returned it. Then I called Dad.

"Hey, Pop, is everything okay?" He had no time for chitchat.

"Yeah. The horses are fine, and I just got back from Scarborough's. Storm actually seemed calm today, and I fed him and just stood watching him for a little bit. I took Beau along with me."

"Did it look like anyone had been there to mess with anything?" I asked, thinking of the snakes. That still stuck with me, and while it could have been a prank, it seemed over the top for something like that to me.

"No. I thought about that and I've been listening, but haven't heard anything. I did call a buddy at the auction house, but he insists there was nothing unusual about the sale. The former owners are damned hard to track down, but I'm trying. And I set indicators throughout the ranch, so if anyone does show up here, I'll know. This whole thing has me jittery."

"Both of us too," I agreed.

"I'll be back tonight, and I'll send you a message if I find anything." He seemed pretty happy. "Come on, Beau, it's time for us to go," he said to the dog. "Have a good day, boy, and be safe." He ended the call, and I put the phone on the bedside table.

When Scarborough joined me, I told him that things were good at home, and we watched television without talking for a little while until it was time to get ready. He seemed deep in thought, and I didn't want to bother him.

Scarborough looked nice in tan pants and a blue-and-red-striped polo shirt. I checked myself in the mirror, making sure I hadn't forgotten anything. Then we left and walked down the main street to the pub.

"You made it," Buddy said, with a gorgeous lady standing next to him. "This is Gwen. Gwen, this is Scarry and his friend Martin."

She took Scarborough's hand. "I've heard so much about you." Her smile was genuine. "I'm so glad I got the chance to meet you." She shook my hand afterward as Buddy turned to the room.

"Look who's here," he said, and a number of other guys came over. Most shook Scarborough's hand, a few pulling him into a hug. I stepped back and let Scarborough talk to his friends. A few people were at the bar, and I wandered over, ordered a red beer, and took a seat, swiveling around so I could see what was going on.

"Who are you with?" one of the ladies asked as she took the stool next to mine.

"He's Scarborough's friend," Gwen said, sitting on the other side of me. "They came here from Wyoming."

"Wow, I haven't seen him since school," the lady said. "Hi, and by the way, I'm Iris, married to Chris over there. He was a friend of Scarborough's in school. I was a year behind them." She sipped from her glass, and Gwen ordered a soda water.

"Not drinking?" Iris asked Gwen, and Gwen smiled. Iris put her hand over her mouth. "Congratulations! How far along?"

"Three months." Gwen sipped from her glass again. "This one was a bit of a surprise. The others are ten and seven." She took a deep breath. "This will definitely be the last one. Do you and Chris have kids?"

"Two. They're at home for the evening with my mom," Iris said, and drank some more of her beer. "I love that we live close enough to walk."

"We walked too. The hotel is just down the street," Gwen said, and turned to me. "Are you staying at the Howard House too?"

I nodded, and caught sight of Scarborough in the middle of a group of guys. They were all talking, and Scarborough seemed at ease and damned happy. The energy in the room was so positive, and that had been what I was hoping for. Scarborough deserved that.

"Are you and Scarborough together?" Iris asked.

"We're friends," I answered.

Iris nodded and smirked. "I have a sense for these kinds of things, and you keep looking at him like he's a hot fudge sundae." She winked. "You sure there isn't a little something something?" She smirked again and bumped my shoulder.

Dammit if I didn't blush, and both ladies snickered. "Actually, we're just friends," I said, chuckling to myself.

"But you want there to be more," Iris added.

I couldn't deny it.

Instead, I shrugged and let my gaze wander over to Scarborough once again. This time, he seemed to have found mine as well. He grinned and raised his glass. I nodded and smiled back. Scarborough wound through the people. "We have a table in the back if you all want to come and get something to eat."

We all threaded through the throng of people to the eight-top in the back. Buddy held the chair for Gwen, and Chris joined Iris, while I sat next to Scarborough. "What have you been up to?" Iris asked Scarborough.

"I have a ranch of my own in Wyoming. It isn't very big, but it's perfect for me. I raise cattle and have a few horses. One that could be pretty special once Martin works with him. He's like the local horse whisperer."

"It's just a matter of experience and knowing what they need and how they react," I said gently. "It also takes a lot of patience." There was more to it, but I couldn't put my finger on exactly what it was.

"How so?" Gwen asked. "I grew up in the city."

Scarborough drank his beer and talked to Buddy and Chris.

"Scarborough has a horse that someone really did a number on. He's afraid of just about everyone. But he's totally beautiful.

I'm working to help him rebuild some of the trust of people that was ripped away from him."

"Is he scarred?" Iris asked.

I shook my head. "It's like he was beaten and whipped, but there are no marks. It really makes no sense at all to me." I didn't mention the snakes and things in the paddock because it wasn't germane at the moment. "Physically he's stunning, with great conformation and lines. That's why Scarborough bought him. But the rest is a mystery. We're trying to find out where he came from, but it could be almost anywhere in the country."

Iris nodded. "It could be a mental deficiency of some sort. Horses can get them the same as people. They have personalities just like us. I would have thought a horse that was abused would have marks or be undernourished." She leaned closer. "He could have been experimented on."

"Excuse me?" I asked.

"A test animal of some sort," Iris offered. "I've heard of various projects where they did behavioral testing on various types of animals."

"That never occurred to me. But horses?" I asked. I had heard of monkeys, rabbits, and mice, but I had never heard about testing on horses. "That seems really cruel to me."

Iris sighed. "Yes, it does. But animal testing is often cruel, or at the very least dangerous to the animals. You could have his blood tested, but it might not tell you much now. Whatever they gave him would likely be out of his system, or they could have just done behavior experiments."

This was too much. "How do you know this sort of thing?"

Iris shrugged. "I read things on the internet, and I heard of a place on the other side of the state that was doing some work with animals. I doubt it was a university. They tend to be much more humane."

Scarborough was listening now. "I sure hope that's not what happened to Storm."

I did too, but it made sense. The horse just showed up at auction with no real background information. Maybe the horse was never supposed to leave the research facility. Or maybe this had nothing to do with Storm at all.

"What are you going to do to help him?" Gwen asked.

"Get him to trust me again. He may never be able to be ridden, but like I said, he's stunning, so Scarborough is hoping if we can calm him down, we can breed him." I sighed. "I'd like to find out what I can about him, but barring that, I can only try to get him over what happened. It can be a long process. But my dad was at Scarborough's today, and he said that Storm was calm and eating in his paddock. He was responding to me before we left, so we'll see how things are when we get home."

"Martin is the best," Scarborough said with a soft smile. My breath hitched as he looked at me.

"What can I bring you?" the server asked. She looked a little haggard. We ordered, and she hurried away. The poor girl was probably being run off her feet, and it didn't seem like there was a great deal of other help. The place was packed, and there looked to be only two servers. Still, they got their orders in as another couple sat down.

"Hi, Janelle," Buddy said.

"Are these seats taken?" she asked with a smile.

"They are now," Buddy said. "How are you?" Buddy made introductions all around, and everyone settled in to talk, mostly about old times. I sat back in my chair and let the conversation swirl around me. It wasn't like I knew anyone here, and that was fine. The purpose of the trip was so Scarborough could have fun and maybe connect with some people he hadn't seen in a long time, and that seemed to be a success. I got up from the table for another beer and returned with one for Scarborough as well, receiving a smile when I set the glass beside him.

"Can I ask you something?" Buddy leaned across the table.

"No," Gwen said firmly. "That's tacky and we don't gossip."

It seemed Buddy did, and my hackles raised.

"Why did you leave town so quickly?" Buddy turned to Chris, who nodded. "We were all friends, and then suddenly you were gone, and we never heard anything more from you. It was like you left in a puff of wind." He gulped his beer. "Dude, we missed you."

I had a pretty good idea where this was going, and I could feel Scarborough's anxiety level stretch all the way to the ceiling. "Let's just say that things weren't as happy at home as people might have thought," I interjected, and Buddy turned to me and then back to Scarborough.

"We know your dad is a total shit."

"Buddy!" Gwen snapped.

"But we do. He always was. Did he throw you out or something? You know you could have stayed with me. My parents loved you. There were rumors after you left, and…. You could have stayed with us. That's all. You didn't have to leave."

Scarborough drained his beer in a few gulps, then set the glass on the table. "Your mom and dad would have taken in a gay kid who had just been outed by his father after being caught with another boy?" he asked, meeting the gazes of everyone around the table with a bar of ocular steel. Damn, it was impressive to have him stand up for himself like that. "I… yes… my father kicked me out—or beat me out the door is more like it. I didn't think anyone would have anything to do with me, so I left and did what I'd always done at home—I worked. Did the jobs no one else wanted to do. There were hard times, and I spent a lot of time sleeping in the truck because it was the only shelter I had. But what was I gonna do? Home wasn't an option…." Scarborough's anger seemed to peter out, and he grew quiet once again.

"So you left and didn't come back except for the funeral, and even then you didn't call anyone and left right away?" Buddy seemed genuinely hurt, and in a way, I was glad to see it.

Scarborough had to know that he'd had friends who cared about him, even if he hadn't realized it at the time.

"I didn't think anyone would care after what came out," he said softly.

"Well, we did," Buddy said. "And we're glad you're here now." He patted Scarborough's hand. "Have you seen your dad?"

Scarborough shook his head. "I'm here for the reunion and to see you guys. Once it's over, I'm going back to Wyoming, and I'll be happy if I can get in and out of town without seeing him. He didn't want me then, and I have a life of my own now."

"Okay," Gwen said from next to me. "Why don't we talk about something else? That was a long time ago." She smiled, and Buddy nodded, shifting the topic to basketball, which seemed to make the guys happy and the women near me roll their eyes.

"Oh, the glory days," I sighed, and the women all chuckled.

"They talk about every high school game as though it were the most important thing in their lives," Iris said. "I don't get it." The ladies began talking in earnest, and I drank my beer and was grateful when dinner came. The conversation barely let up for a second, which was fine. The guys relived happy days of heady excitement, and the ladies talked about themselves and what they were doing now. It was like being caught between two worlds, and I didn't mind a bit.

"THAT WAS fun," Scarborough said once we were back in the hotel room. He was more than a little tipsy, and I let him use the bathroom first. Beer was only rented, never bought, and once he was done, I took my turn.

"Did you enjoy seeing your friends?" I asked when I came out.

Scarborough lay back on the bed, his arms spread out, his eyes dropping. "Yeah. I was afraid that no one was going to want to have anything to do with me. Things were so different then." He took a deep breath and lay still. "I honestly thought that none of them were going to care what happened. People are still very conservative here and, well… maybe I jumped to conclusions."

I couldn't blame him, after what his father had done. I probably would have left too. The beer was getting to me, and I figured I should get ready for bed. Since Scarborough stayed put, I used the opportunity to change into a pair of light shorts and clean up. When I emerged from the bathroom, Scarborough hadn't moved. "Come on. You need to clean up and take something so you don't have a headache."

Scarborough groaned as he got up and shuffled to the bathroom. I climbed under the covers and turned out all but one light. When Scarborough came out again, he got in on the other side of the bed, and I turned out the light. "Night, Marty," he said softly.

"Night, Scarry." I couldn't help teasing. Scarborough chuckled softly for about two seconds, and then his breathing evened out and I could tell he was already falling to sleep. I stared up at the ceiling, trying to keep my imagination from running away with me. Scarborough rolled over and drew closer. He was out like a light, but his closeness definitely had parts of me awake and raring to go. God, this was going to be harder than I thought in so many ways. I needed to keep it together for another two days, and then we'd be on our way home and back to normal.

CHAPTER 6

SOMETHING WAS off, and yet damned pleasant. I tried not to think about it as I hovered on the precipice between wake and sleep. I was warm, but not too warm, like cozy and comfortably warm. If I put my arm outside the covers, the chill from the air-conditioning had me putting it back. I let myself sink into happy sleep, pushing against the solid wall behind me, an arm resting around my waist. I sighed and tried to remember who was in the bed with me.

My eyes snapped open, and even though the room was still dark, I didn't need to see to know that Scarborough was right behind me, pressed against me. Instantly my body went on alert and I was hard as stone. From the feeling just behind me and the way Scarborough shimmied slowly against me, he was exactly the same. Oh yeah… I knew that delicious hardness against my ass. Part of me knew I should move away and just pretend this hadn't happened and that things were normal and unchanged. But damn, it felt so good.

Scarborough mumbled something in his sleep that sounded like my name and then pressed even closer. I hoped he was still asleep. Maybe he was dreaming of me. I wondered what I should do, and in the end, slowly moved away and rolled over, just so I could watch him. Not that there was much light to see anything. Our room was in the back, so there was no light from the street to shine in the window.

He was definitely asleep and settled quietly again, but his arm reached out and eventually wrapped around his pillow before quieting once more. *Okay, I can do this.* I moved back on the bed to put more space between us and tried again to sleep.

I woke to the same sensation, only this time there was a gentle glow shining around the curtains. And that same pressure against my backside and warmth and comfort enveloped me. This time, when I tried to move away, Scarborough drew me closer for a few seconds, and then he stopped and gasped. "I'm sorry," he whispered, and rolled over, turning to face the far wall. "I was asleep, I didn't...."

"It's okay," I said softly, because it had been damned nice and a long time since I had been cuddled by anyone. Sex was mostly... well, quickies in dark places when on the circuit, and in Red Rock... okay, the Mojave Desert had nothing on my dry spell. "I mean, you were sleeping and...." I tried to make him feel better and give him an out, when every fiber of my being told me to just jump him. Roll Scarborough back over to face me, slide closer, and see exactly what that luscious body of his felt like on top of me, under me, dammit, I didn't care.

"I didn't mean to molest you in your sleep or anything." Scarborough pushed back the covers and got out of the bed. I wondered what I should do and figured he was going to the bathroom. Instead, the movement in the room ceased, and when I rolled over, I found Scarborough sitting in the chair with one of the discarded bedcovers pulled over him. What the hell was he doing?

"You weren't," I told him with a sigh. "What time is it?"

"A little before seven," Scarborough answered. "I should probably get up. There's breakfast down in the dining room. I could eat and get out of your hair, and...." He yawned.

"Or you could get back in the bed and get some rest. We were out late last night, and I doubt there's going to be an early night tonight either. You also have a basketball game later this morning with the guys." I had no intention of missing that.

65

"But…."

I pulled back the covers, and he sighed, dropped the coverlet, and got back into the bed. He stayed way on the far side, clinging to the mattress. "You said my name in your sleep," I said.

"No, I didn't," he countered, and I didn't press him, but smiled. "You're teasing me."

"Nope. You did."

Scarborough groaned.

"I liked it," I told him, waiting for his reaction.

"What?" He rolled over. "You liked me saying your name, which I didn't… or molesting you in your sleep?" He closed his eyes, and I gently touched his chin.

"Let's get something straight, right now. You didn't molest me. You held me, and it was nice. And yes, you said my name, which was equally nice, because it meant you were dreaming about me." I lay on my back, my hands under my head, staring up at the flowered plaster ceiling medallion. I waited to see what Scarborough would say, but the room was still other than the hum of the air conditioner. "Who told you that touching someone was molesting them?"

"My father… the guy I was caught with. He said that it was all my fault and that…." Scarborough grew quiet, and I rolled over and slid closer to him.

"They were wrong," I told him. "It's that simple. I know you well enough to know that you would never do anything against anyone's will. You wouldn't coerce anyone into anything."

"But he said, and…." The pain rang in Scarborough's voice.

"He had just been caught with another guy, and he blamed the whole thing on you. And your father and mother let him. After what he did to you, your dad isn't a reliable source for anything, and neither is this young man who was too chickenshit to stand up for the truth." I slid even nearer and drew Scarborough closer. "You can't molest someone when they want you." I stroked along Scarborough's jaw as his phone rang next to the bed. Scarborough jumped back, and I sighed, flopping into the pillow while he took the call.

"No. I don't particularly want to see you," Scarborough said anxiously, his posture suddenly rigid. "No, I haven't been in touch with you in fifteen years, and that was my choice." He rocked slightly as he sat. "No. I don't owe you anything. You made my life hell and you said I wasn't your son any longer, so I left and made my own way." He continued to listen and leaned forward, his head lowering. I could only imagine that he was talking to his father. How he got Scarborough's number, I wasn't sure, unless someone associated with the reunion passed it on. It was a small town, so sometimes information tended to get around, particularly if you were trying to find it.

"It's okay. You don't have to talk to him if you don't want," I whispered to Scarborough.

He nodded but didn't put the phone down. "That isn't my problem. My place is a success because I work hard to make it that way, and I'm not sending you anything." The voice on the other side of the line grew loud enough that I could hear it.

"You owe me. I raised you and—"

"No. You kicked me out when you found out something you didn't like." Scarborough huffed. "I'm going to go now, and don't call me again. I'm going to block this number and will not be taking any more of your calls. I wish you good luck with the farm and your debt problem, but I'm not bailing you out." He hung up and dropped the phone on the bed, holding his head in his hands.

"Your dad?" I asked, and Scarborough nodded, confirming my suspicion. "I take it he wanted money."

"Yeah. The farm is deeply in debt, and he heard I was in town, so he decided to try to guilt me into helping him." He sighed, and I could tell he was majorly conflicted. No matter what he had done to him, he was still his father, and Scarborough was loyal enough that saying no must have been difficult for him. "I worked so hard to build my own life and to make it stable. I've scrimped and saved every cent I have, and I'm supposed to throw it away on someone who didn't want me." He swallowed, and the mood from earlier was most clearly gone.

I nodded and thought I knew what he was thinking. It would be so easy to hope that if he did this that his father would welcome him with open arms and accept him for who he was. It wasn't rational, but just that kernel of hope could send someone into a tailspin.

"I know he would never accept me, and I thought I had come to terms with that a long time ago. But now I think I was always holding out hope that he might change his mind."

That he was so shook up just went to prove the kind of heart that Scarborough had. His exterior might be thick, but he had a heart… and as it turned out, a bigger one than I ever thought. See, I think if it had been me, I would have told the old man to go screw himself six ways from Sunday. Scarborough would have been within his rights to do that, but instead he was agonizing over his decision. I hated to see him this way.

"No. It's only the money that interests him. Not anything else." At least that was how it looked to me. "I'm sorry."

Scarborough lifted his gaze from the floor. "Me too." He shrugged. "There's nothing I can do to help them. Dad needs more money than I can provide anyway." He straightened up and then stood to head to the bathroom. "It just sucks that the first time I speak to him in years is because he wants money." He went inside and closed the door.

I wanted to wring Scarborough's father's neck, but it was likely I was never going to meet the man. While I waited for Scarborough to shower and clean up, I messaged Dad to see how things were going and received a thumbs-up in response. Even in his texts, Dad didn't say much. When Scarborough was done, I took my turn, and once I was alone in the bathroom, I tried not to think of how close things had come between us. I could kill his father for calling so damned early in the morning. Not only had he put the guilty number on Scarborough, the man had fucking cockblocked him without knowing it. I showered and dressed, then joined Scarborough.

"Look, I'm sorry about this morning. I was dreaming and things got out of hand and…. Maybe I was just hungover and not thinking clearly…."

I drew closer. "I'm not sorry for anything… well, except maybe your father's timing. But as far as you and me…." I walked around the bed and leaned over where Scarborough was sitting. "I'm not sorry for a damned thing that happened in bed." His eyes grew wide and his breath hitched. "I'm hoping that after we get back from the reunion, and if it isn't too late, that we can see where things take us."

"But you're my friend…," Scarborough whispered.

"And sometimes friends make the best lovers," I retorted. He gasped, and I came nearer. "Did you like holding me in bed?"

Scarborough nodded.

"And what did you think about me holding you, being close? Did you like that?" Damn, I knew he did, because I had felt just how much and how excited Scarborough was. "Then just let things happen."

"Are you sure?" Scarborough asked.

"Yes. Don't let what happened to you all those years ago stop you from at least being open to making yourself happy." I leaned even closer and tilted my head to kiss him gently.

Damn, the first taste of Scarborough only made me want more—a hell of a lot more. But that wasn't in the cards for now. Besides, judging by the spooked look in Scarborough's eyes, I knew if I pushed it, he'd bolt like an unbroken colt. So I backed away to give him some breathing room.

"Come on. Let's go get some breakfast, and then we can find this place where you're supposed to meet your friends and play basketball." I turned and let him think over what just happened.

And damn, was he cute, with his huge puppy-dog eyes, filling with hope that he was probably fighting with everything he had. But I figured, fuck it all. If Mom was going to put these kinds of ideas in my head and I couldn't let them go, then let's see what happened.

Of course, it could all backfire and Scarborough could simply bury himself deeper. But I hoped not. He was discovering some things about his past that likely weren't what he had been expecting. So maybe something new in Scarborough's present life wasn't such a bad idea. It was up to him and whether he was willing to open himself to it. All I could do was wait and see.

"Come on." I patted his shoulder, and he finally stood, and we headed downstairs.

GWEN AND Buddy apparently had come down just before us, and we joined their table. "Did you sleep well?" Gwen asked, and Scarborough blushed. Gwen tittered softly. "I see."

"No. It wasn't like that. There were supposed to be two beds, but those rooms were full." I smirked. "And he snores. Like, loud enough to wake the dead." I winked.

"I do not, and if anyone snores, it's you." Scarborough rolled his eyes. "I swear I needed earplugs. You lay on your back and my God." He sipped from the glass of juice, and I noticed Buddy and Gwen giving each other knowing looks. I let them pass, got up, and filled a plate from the buffet table. Eggs, bacon, sausage, even pancakes. There was plenty to eat, and for some reason, I was starved. When I returned, Scarborough was still at the table talking with Buddy, the two of them going on about basketball and sports in general.

"He never says a lot to anyone," I told Gwen. Hell, in all the years I'd known him, I think Scarborough had never said that much to me in all that time, and here he was, chatting away like a social butterfly.

She shrugged. "It happens with old friends." She seemed pleased, and I tucked into my breakfast. Eventually the others filled their plates, with Buddy and Scarborough barely taking a break from their conversation. It made me wonder. Scarborough and I were friends, but maybe we didn't have enough in common. Clearly he and Buddy did. They seemed to be able to talk for hours, and yet I knew Scarborough as a typical closemouthed cowboy, like my father.

"Sorry to monopolize the conversation," Buddy said, about the time I finished eating. Scarborough was happy, and I shrugged. They had things to talk about and plenty to catch up on. Buddy put his napkin on the table, and Gwen did the same. "We're going to go back to the room. Do you want to meet in the lobby in fifteen minutes and we can go over to the game together?"

I shared a glance with Scarborough before nodding. "That would be great." They left, and I waited for Scarborough to finish. "Do you need to change into basketball duds?"

Scarborough looked down at what he was wearing. "I need to change my shoes." He left the table and went upstairs.

I finished my coffee and joined the others in the lobby, waiting just a minute for Scarborough to come down. Then the four of us rode to the park in Buddy's rental car.

"Hey, there they are," a tall man said as we got out of the car. A basketball came sailing in our direction, and Scarborough snatched it out of the air and beaned it back. Both of them smiled, and Buddy and Scarborough headed over to join the rest of the group.

"There's a bench over there in the shade," I offered, and Gwen and I headed that way to take a seat.

"This is so good for him," Gwen said. "Buddy has been looking forward to seeing his old friends for weeks. He works too hard, and the pressure is something else." She waved, and Buddy waved back, one of the guys giving him a teasing shove.

"It's good for Scarborough too," I agreed, though I didn't go into my reasons why. Scarborough's business was his own, and I wasn't going to tell tales on him.

The guys divided into teams, and then the one side took off their shirts. Gwen and I hooted at them, and the guys preened for her—I was pretty sure—and then set about their game. Most of the guys seemed to have let themselves go a little over the years, but I found my gaze following Scarborough as he moved up and down the court. Damn, without his shirt on, he was some sort of sex god.

A few others joined us, and I stood to make room on the bench. The sun warmed the day and the competition on the court heated as well. It wasn't long before old habits and rivalries took hold once again—blocking became more aggressive, shots a little more desperate.

More than the game, I was mesmerized by the way Scarborough's skin glistened with sweat and how he seemed to move with a fluid grace I never knew he possessed.

"He's something else," Beth, one of the fascinated women, said.

I nodded. I had no idea who she was talking about, and I didn't care. Scarborough was something else, and I was glad no one could see just how exciting that idea truly was. "Damn," I breathed, not taking my gaze away from the court.

"Don't drool," Gwen said from next to me, and I closed my mouth and swallowed, because yeah, I had been about two seconds from it and had no idea. "Are you sure there's nothing between you?"

Scarborough jumped, making a layup, his body elongating, movements as fluid as a dancer I'd seen on television. *Holy cow.* The women nearby grew quiet, and when I turned, they were all watching Scarborough as well.

"Too bad he doesn't swing my way… because…," one of the women whispered, and I smiled, wishing I could say he was mine, even as a bit of jealousy reared forward.

I turned to the group. "Okay, I have to ask… are you all really that accepting? I was ready to fight God knows what to ensure he had a good time, but everyone has been so nice. Well, except his father, who's apparently a selfish jackass. Things can be pretty conservative where we're from, and I was expecting the same thing here."

Gwen shrugged and turned to the others. "We're from Washington, and it's no big deal. I don't think it ever mattered to Buddy."

"Folks can be pretty Bible Belty here, no doubt. Our preacher says that love is what counts and that hating people is wrong." Beth grinned. "But not everyone feels that way. There will be people who will stay away from y'all at the reunion, and maybe some will refuse to talk to Scarborough. Who knows? There better not be any trouble." She smiled and pointed to a huge guy standing in the shade just at the end of the court. "That's Harv, my husband. He worked as a bouncer at a bar in Omaha. Nothing is going to happen on his watch."

"I see." I guess it was good to know people who were as big as a house.

"Mostly people will be quiet and polite, and then they'll talk about you behind your back, because that's what we do." Sharon giggled. "But you'll be gone anyway, so it really doesn't matter. And the folks here will have met some nice gay people and seen that they don't have two heads and a forked tongue." She smiled a wicked grin. "You don't, do you?"

"Sharon," Iris said with mock scandalization as I stuck out my tongue and then smiled. The game seemed to be done, and the guys on Scarborough's team clapped one another on the shoulders while the rest trooped off the court.

"Did you win?" I asked as he approached, trying to put his shirt back on, but it didn't want to go. I jogged over and helped him pull it down in the back, running my hand lightly over the sweaty muscles.

"We killed them." He turned to me with a grin. "It's good to know I still have some moves." He whirled around as his shirt fell into place. "I didn't realize how much I missed things like this."

I nodded, and we joined the group congregating around the ladies. "Then you need to do it more often," I mentioned, and Scarborough shook his head, which seemed strange to me. He obviously loved playing and he was good at it. I didn't understand why he didn't want to play. There were groups of guys who shot hoops in the park back home almost all the time.

"This is like vacation—back home is work," he said with a tone that said the subject was closed.

"Water or soda?" one of the guys asked, popping open a cooler, and everyone got what they wanted. It was a nice morning, with a breeze flowing through the expansive limbs overhead that shaded much of the park. "Anyone up for another game?"

The guys finished their drinks and treated us to another show of their skill. This time they were a man short, and it seemed I was being drafted.

"Good God," I said, hobbling into the hotel room and collapsing on the bed. "You guys play for keeps." My legs ached something fierce. "I work outside all the time, but that was…."

"I know. It used different muscles." Scarborough handed me a couple of pills and a glass of water. "I'm feeling it too. Guess I'm not as young as I used to be."

I took the pills and lay back, closing my eyes and hoping they took effect quickly, because I didn't remember feeling like this after an entire day in the saddle. "None of us is. How long has it been since you played?" I asked.

"High school. I never had time once I left home. There was always work to do, and I needed to worry about where my next meal was coming from." He lay down on the other side of the bed. "This is definitely a game for people younger than me."

"I don't think so. Like you said, we're using muscles that we don't usually work. If you played regularly, you wouldn't feel this way."

"No. I'd be too damned tired to get my real work done." He sighed, and I didn't argue. He was entitled to his opinion, and I was too pooped to put up any sort of fight. Instead, I lay where I was, listening to the air conditioner and soaking up the cool air.

"What time is the reunion?" I asked.

"It starts with cocktails and drinks at five thirty, with dinner at seven. Apparently there's going to be dancing as well. But…."

"I can two-step," I offered. "Mom taught me various dances when I was growing up. She insisted that any man who could dance was more likely to catch himself a wife. She said that the way to a man's heart was through his stomach, and the way to a woman's was on the dance floor. That was before she knew I was gay. Still, I doubt it would have mattered. She was determined that I not have two left feet." I wagged my eyebrows.

Scarborough scoffed. "Do you really think the people here are ready to see two men dancing together? I somehow doubt it." Still, he smiled and seemed to like the idea. "I don't honestly see any need to rub anyone's nose in the fact that I'm gay. I can have a good time at the reunion and not make a big deal about the whole gay thing. Then we can go home and back to our lives."

"Is that what you really want to do?" I asked. "You've had a great time with your friends. Do you really want to go back home and have everything be the way it was?" That didn't make sense to me. Scarborough had gotten a taste of fun and people who liked him. Hell, the guy had been social, something he never was at home, other than maybe when Mom had him over for dinner.

"I can't stay here. A visit is one thing, but I don't want to come back here."

"That's not what I meant." I sighed and closed my eyes. Scarborough had completely misunderstood my meaning, and now he was way off track.

"Oh…. Well… there's still plenty to do at home and this is a nice break, but there isn't a lot of time for things like this. I have a ranch to run." He sat up and went into the bathroom, cutting off further conversation.

My phone buzzed and I answered it. "Hey, Dad."

"I'm at Scarborough's and someone has been here. A few of my indicators were tripped. I checked out everything, and it doesn't seem like any of the animals were tampered with and all the paddock doors were still closed. Tell Scarborough that I'm going to bring all the horses inside the barn and lock it up. They're calling for storms to come through this afternoon and evening, so I'm battening things down."

"I'll tell him, and just be careful of Storm. I don't know how he'll react."

"Oh, him. He's okay. I fed him today and he was fine. He's already inside one of the stalls and is eating and drinking like a champ. The sun has been so fierce that I brought him in this morning to get him out of the heat. Tell Scarborough that I'm watching things closely." He seemed as confident as ever. "That horse is really something special, and I think that someone is going to be very upset that they let him go. He's calm and acting much more normal than he was a few days ago. It's like whatever was in his system has worked its way out." That maybe gave some credence to what Iris had said about animal testing earlier.

"Thanks, Dad. Have you got your horses in my barn?"

"Yes. They're content alongside yours. But that dog of yours keeps wandering around looking for you," Dad said.

"We'll be back in a few days, and then he'll be happy."

"Be safe," Dad said, and ended the call.

I told Scarborough what Dad had said once he came out of the bathroom.

"I wish I knew what was up with that horse," Scarborough said.

I nodded. "What in the hell could they want? I mean, they could try to steal the horse back, but I doubt they'd get very far. If he's truly valuable, then we need to figure out where he came from." I kept wondering how we could trace him. There were many ways to hide a horse's lineage and background. There were plenty of horses in the US who were born, used, and never left a farm. And it wasn't like Storm had particular skills. He wasn't a dressage horse or a racer. There were detailed records on those types of animals. "Iris said something about him being a test animal, and I keep going back to that. What if someone was doing some sort of experiments on him and that's why he's so freaked out about things?"

"But why sell him, then?"

I turned to Scarborough. "I don't know. Maybe he wasn't meant to be sold. What if that part was an accident and they weren't done with him, but he was taken off to auction, sold, and that was the end of it?" I shrugged. This was all conjecture and based on absolutely nothing at all other than my imagination, which immediately skipped tracks as Scarborough sat down in the chair. "You know, you looked pretty amazing playing today. All the ladies were damned jealous." I grinned, and Scarborough rolled his eyes as though he didn't believe me. "They all said that if you swung their way, they'd take a ride on your trapeze." I chuckled when Scarborough snorted. "I'm not kidding." I stood and walked over to him. "You were damned hot." I leaned on the arm of the chair, holding Scarborough's gaze as heat rose in his eyes. His breathing hitched, and I could almost feel his temperature rising.

"You should get cleaned up." Scarborough swallowed hard, and I moved away. "We're supposed to meet some of the guys for lunch at the diner down the street."

"Okay…." It hurt to be rejected when we had been so close earlier. "I'll go get cleaned up." Straightening, I turned toward the bathroom.

"Marty," Scarborough said, getting out of the chair. "I'm not turning you down," he said softly. "I don't know how to do this. It's been a very long time since I was with anyone, and after that, my life fell apart. I work and I work; that's pretty much my life." He paused and came closer. "Just give me a few hours to get my mind around all of this, and then I can think about everything more clearly. Because right now, my mind is all about you and how you make me feel. But I don't know what to do with it." He put his hand on my shoulder. "Just give me a little time."

LUNCH WITH Scarborough's friends was fun for him. I talked to a few people, ate, and did my best not to seem too bored. Scarborough's attention was where it should have been—on his friends and the people he'd come to see. Afterward, I returned to the hotel, and Scarborough and some friends decided to explore the town to see what had changed.

The bed in the room was comfortable enough, and I lay on it, feet up, watching television. Time to do nothing was a luxury as far as I was concerned, and I decided that I'd take advantage of a few hours of rest. It would have been nice to have had Scarborough with me. I smiled at the idea of having someone to do nothing with, but….

"Hey," Scarborough said, coming in about three in the afternoon and closing the door behind him.

"Did you have a good time with your friends?" I asked, placing my hands behind my head. I was about to reach for the remote, but Scarborough kicked off his shoes and lay down next to me.

"It was fun. Not much has changed around here, except some of the downtown is empty now. Buddy said that the town is trying to encourage new businesses, but it's pretty hard for them." He sighed. "I remember walking from the school to the drugstore at lunch. Thankfully it's still there, but the Ben Franklin is gone, and so are a few other stores I remember."

"I suppose that's what happens over time." I groaned and closed my eyes. The quiet and downtime were catching up with me.

"Yeah, I guess...." Scarborough breathed.

I rolled onto my side, propping my head in my hand. "Are you glad you came?"

"Yeah." Scarborough turned to face me. "You're a good friend, I know that."

I felt a *but* coming on.

"But you're my friend, and I don't want to mess that up. If we... you know... it's going to change everything, and what if stuff doesn't work out? Our friendship will be over, and how can I face you or anyone else?" He blinked. "I don't have many friends at home, and I can't lose the ones I have." I got a glimpse of a scared boy in those huge blue eyes.

I couldn't argue with that. Sex changed things, but each time I inhaled, I could smell his deep scent, and it drew me closer. I knew what it felt like to be held in his arms, and I wanted that again. Sometimes life just sucked big-time. "If that's how you feel...."

"It doesn't matter what I feel. I have to do what I think is right. My feelings are completely secondary. If I let my feelings guide everything in my life, then I'd end up right back where I was when Mom and Dad kicked me out. I was a complete mess, with no idea where to turn and no place to go, and I can't go back to feeling all alone like that."

I reached out and put my hand against the center of his chest. "You've been living in your head for so long, you don't know what else to do. I get that. But there is so much more to life than just that." I scooted closer. "I'm your friend, and I'll always be your friend. It doesn't matter if something happens between us or not. I'm not going to stop being your friend because of it. But what really matters is what you want, not what you think you should do." I wasn't going to pressure him, but my heart raced just having him this close. "No one can live in just their head all the time. Sometimes you have to let your heart guide you too."

I sat up and slipped off the bed. I'd said what I needed to, and yeah, I was disappointed, but as I had told Scarborough, I wasn't going to let that interfere with our friendship. There were still a few hours until we had to leave for the reunion, and I thought it was my turn to go for a walk.

"Where are you going?" he asked.

"I'll be back in time for the reunion." I pulled open the room door and stepped into the warm hallway. I needed some time to calm down and let my head and heart settle. If Scarborough wasn't interested in me, then there was nothing I could do about it.

The sun was bright and strong as I went out of the front door of the hotel, heading toward town. For fuck's sake, I was a cowboy, not some pimply teenager. I knew who I was, and I was *so* not going to do the teenage-angsty thing. Scarborough was my friend, and maybe this was for the best.

My phone rang, and I pulled it out. "Hey, Mom." Just the person I wanted to talk to.

"Are you and Scarborough doing okay?" There was a slight giggle in her voice.

"Yes, Mom. He and I are fine. The reunion is doing well for him. He's been able to reconnect with his friends. His dad has hit him up for money." I swallowed hard. "All in all, it's been just hunky-dory."

"Oh… I think someone took his pissy pills," she retorted. "What's wrong, did he turn you down?"

"Mother," I said carefully, "I am not going to talk to you about... that kind of stuff."

"Oh, piffle. How are you ever going to find someone without my help? You and your father are completely helpless when it comes to that sort of thing. That man is perfect for you, and if he's unsure, then you might need to put in a little more effort. Don't just expect to bat those baby blues of yours and waggle those rodeo hips and expect everyone to swoon over you."

God, I was about to swallow my teeth. "Mom."

She laughed at me. "Scarborough has been little more than a hermit for the entire time you've known him. Do you remember how you got to be his friend?"

"Yeah," I said and groaned.

"Part of his barn fell down after he bought the place, and the man was building the new one on his own. You went over to help, and it took two days of work before he said more to you than 'good morning' and bothered to offer you a drink, while he worked full tilt so you wouldn't have to help him anymore."

"Yeah, I know. It takes a while for him to warm up to anyone." I knew that.

Mom groaned. "You men are so stupid sometimes. Your father is the exact same way. Scarborough is so worried about relying on other people because if he doesn't need them, then they can't let him down. He didn't talk to you much for days because he expected you to disappear just like everyone else had. Instead, you came every day, because you and your father are both like mules... and you wore him down. He came to trust you, and then you could be friends." She cleared her throat, and I heard the clink of ice cubes in the background. I could just picture Mom drinking her sweet tea. "My guess is that he counts on your friendship for more than you can know. It's a lot bigger for him than it is for you because you have other friends."

"I guess." What Mom said made sense.

81

"No guessing. He has more to lose than you do," Mom said. "Anyway, have you talked to your father lately?"

"This morning, why?"

"O-kay. He's been busy moving horses around. He chased someone off Scarborough's, must have been just after he talked to you. So your father walked that new horse of his across the fields and down to our place. You were right—he's beautiful. And now he's in our barn, and your father rode one of our horses to Scarborough's. We figured we'd hide him for a while and see what happens. Your dad was going to call Scarborough, but he probably forgot." She hummed, and I could suddenly hear the tension in her voice. "A storm is coming up, and that stubborn mule is still out there. I'll talk to you later. I have to go make sure he's okay. This is going to be a gully washer."

"Okay. Thanks, Mom, for everything." I waited for her to hang up and then turned around and went back toward the hotel, pulling up the radar on my phone as I went. The line of storms was intense, and there was a severe storm warning for home, but thankfully no tornado alerts. That was a small favor, anyway.

"Looks like we're in for rain back home," I said as I returned to the room.

"That's good." Scarborough was still in the same place, with the TV on, but I doubted he was actually watching it. "We need it pretty badly. The creek was really low."

"Has Dad called you?" I asked, and Scarborough sat up, reaching for his phone.

"Dang." He got off the bed, rummaged through his bag to find the cord, and plugged it in. "It's dead." At least that explained it.

"Dad ran someone off at your place, so Mom said, and he moved Storm into their barn and put one of their horses in yours. Apparently he walked Storm through the fields to get there." That was quite a distance. "That should keep him safe until we get home."

Scarborough's phone powered up and began beeping with messages of various kinds. "I had expected to go home on Monday, but maybe we should leave tomorrow."

"If that's what you want to do, let the hotel know right away." I wasn't sure if they would charge us for the night tomorrow or not. "We can pack in the morning and go."

Scarborough jumped up and left the room, probably to check down at the desk. I began getting my things together and laying out what I planned to wear tonight. It wasn't that either of us were slobs, but it seemed like a good idea to get things packed. It helped get my head around the idea. Once he got back and informed me that we were all set, we began changing for the evening's festivities.

THE ORGANIZING committee had decorated the Grange hall in the blue and gold school colors. It was tasteful and quite nice. Scarborough was nervous, and we found a table after making a stop for beer at the bar.

"Go ahead and talk to people. I'll stay here for a little while." I was still a little sore from basketball, and it felt good to sit down for a few minutes.

"Are you sure?" he asked.

I nodded. "Don't worry about me. I'm fine, and I'm sure some of the ladies will show up later and we can all talk. This is your reunion, and I'm here for you. So have a good time." I smiled, and he wandered off toward a group of guys, glancing back to catch my smile.

"Sending him off on his own," Gwen said as she pulled out a chair.

"Yes. Scarborough is... well... a little closed off in real life. I think this reunion has been really good for him."

She nodded. "But you're afraid he'll revert to type."

Of course I was. Nothing had happened here that was particularly lasting. Scarborough had had a good time and reconnected with friends he hadn't seen in many years. But he'd also go right back to his old ways when he got back home. Scarborough had already as good as told me that.

I shrugged, since there was nothing I could do about that. It didn't mean that I wasn't disappointed, because dammit, I liked the Scarborough I'd seen the last few days—the one who smiled and laughed with his friends. Not that I didn't like the Scarborough I knew from home, but I never really thought of that man as anything more than a friend. This Scarborough got my attention and made me want to know what made him tick, what he thought, and what he'd be like between the sheets. I could also imagine the amazing sounds and the sight of this Scarborough in the throes of passion. Just the idea sent a wave of heat racing up and down my back. Honestly, it was going to be hard to give up this Scarborough for the one I knew back home.

I went on a drink run for the ladies and returned to the table to pass out glasses. The beer was good, and I sipped from the glass, looking across the room, which was growing more and more crowded by the minute. Still, I easily found Scarborough, and he met my gaze. I wasn't sure what I was seeing at first, but then heat grew in his eyes, and when I licked my lips, he did the same. Holy shit, my imagination made a leap, and I wondered if a certain hotel roommate might be changing his mind.

The crowd shifted slightly and Scarborough disappeared from sight. I turned to the others with a sigh. I wasn't necessarily interested in them seeing my confusion, so I schooled my expression.

"Are you a real cowboy?" one of the ladies asked, noticing the hat that I had stowed under my chair. My mom would kill me if I wore it at the table.

"Yes. I rode rodeo for a few years, and I have a number of buckles. I came close in a few big rodeos, but I was never good enough to ride with the big boys." Still, it had been a thrill to stare down and then ride down a bronco or bull, though bronc was my usual event. I had been smaller then, and now I was too big for bulls. "I work with horses most of the time, and I love to ride almost more than anything else." I flashed her a smile. "Are you part of the class?"

"Yeah. Eileen Studer, now Carlson. Unfortunately, my husband is traveling in New York at the moment, so he couldn't be here." She really seemed disappointed and a little down. "He was supposed to come, but his flight was canceled, so he's stuck there for an extra day."

"We're glad you're here," one of the other ladies said as they gave her a hug, and suddenly they were off down memory lane, so I returned my attention to my beer and tried to engage the others in conversation.

The chair next to me pulled back, and Scarborough sat down, bumping my shoulder. "You okay?"

"Yes," I said with forced brightness. I had talked to a few of the people I was getting to know, but mostly there wasn't a lot here for me. I kept telling myself that this wasn't my gathering, it was Scarborough's, and I was determined to make the best of it for him and not act like a bored teenager.

"Good. Dinner is going to start, and then there'll be the welcome and a few speeches, I guess." He rolled his eyes. "Apparently they're giving some awards, and then the music will begin." He rubbed his hands together, and sure enough, the plates were brought out—smoky, rich barbecue. I had had this kind of food before, but the smoke seemed extra enhanced, and I waited for everyone at the table to get their plates, my fingers itching to dig in.

Damn, it was lick-your-fingers spicy and rich.

"They got Dean Cartwell to cater the reunion. He has the best barbecue for miles, and though he retired a few years ago, he came out for the reunion," Eileen explained. "The food alone was worth coming here for. I didn't think I would ever have this again."

85

The meal was clearly meaningful to everyone. "The first time I ever got to eat out was at Mr. Cartwell's," Scarborough whispered to me. "It only happened a few times because it was with friends. Dad never went anywhere but home to eat."

I bumped his shoulder, and we shared a smile as I continued eating some of the most amazing food ever. The richness of the meat and spices burst on my tongue, along with the sides of salad and the best potato salad ever, with bacon, onion, a hint of garlic, and possibly scallion. It was amazing and I wanted more… definitely more.

I finished my dinner, my lips singing from the spices and my hands lickably delicious. When I turned to Scarborough, it was clear he was in beef and hog heaven, his eyes dancing and his leg shaking under the table.

"I'd forgotten about this."

"The next time you come over, I'm going to make you some of my barbecue. It isn't the same as this, but Dad and I have our own secret recipe, and it's really good. I like this, so maybe I can add some of this flavor to what we do."

Dessert followed—a simple cake with ice cream—and then the speeches and presentations, then the music. I asked Eileen if she wanted to dance, and she and I hit the floor. She was a stunning partner, and I guided her around the floor with ease. Then each of the ladies decided they wanted a turn. I barely got a breather all night as lady after lady seemed to line up. Mom was right about the dancing, I had to admit.

Toward the end of the evening, most people were talking and drinking, and I was tired. Scarborough sat talking as I approached the table.

"Are you going to take this man for spin?" Gwen asked.

"Somehow I don't think Nebraska is ready for that," I told her with a smile. I would have loved nothing more than to be able to dance with Scarborough, but it really wasn't in the cards.

Gwen got a wicked smile. "Iris, do you want to dance?" The two women stood and headed to the floor. Eileen, who seemed to have been listening, turned to the friend next to her, and they stood before joining them. It seemed I was being given cover if I wanted to do this.

Cowboy up, Martin, and have the guts, I told myself, and got to my feet. "Scarborough, let's you and me show these people how it's done." I held out my hand, and he hesitated, turning to look at me, probably checking if I'd lost my mind.

"You're serious?"

"As a heart attack. I want to dance with you." I waited until he slowly got to his feet and then took him into my arms and led him into a simple country two-step. The ladies all smiled as we passed them on the floor. A few other lady couples got up to dance, and to my shock, another two men danced together as well. When I saw them take the floor, I was finally able to relax and let my attention center on Scarborough.

"You really are a good dancer," he whispered. "I'm terrible and just hope I don't step on your feet or trip."

"It's okay, just follow me and go where I go. This is an easy dance. Take small steps or just shuffle along." I smiled and gazed deeply into his eyes.

"I'm nervous," he admitted.

"No need to be. We have plenty of support, and it doesn't matter that there are a few people who seem to be pointedly ignoring what's going on." I chuckled. "Buddy has picked himself up a partner and they're now dancing." I turned Scarborough so he could see, and his smile said all I needed to know.

"You have guts," Scarborough said. "I'll give you that."

"And I can be one tenacious bastard when I want something." I didn't lean in to kiss him, but we connected with our eyes. "You need to know that." The music continued, and I turned Scarborough again. "I've wondered what you would feel like in my arms for a while, and now I get to find out." We continued moving, and then the song ended and moved into a slower one. The couples on the floor shifted, and I wasn't sure if Scarborough would move closer, but it seemed a number of couples had come to the floor. They formed a circle around us, sort of protecting and showing their support. Scarborough did indeed move nearer, and I held him around the waist, the two of us swaying and moving to the music.

"Have you ever danced... like this before?" Scarborough asked softly.

"You mean, with another guy? Not really. The guys I was with before, they weren't interested in dancing or anything much other than getting right down to it." I leaned closer. "You smell really good." Tightening my hold just a little, I closed my eyes and let the music, the feel of Scarborough in my arms, and his intoxicating scent carry me along.

"People are watching us," Scarborough whispered.

"If you want to stop, just let me know and we can go back to the table." That was Scarborough's call. The stubborn cowboy inside me said that no one was going to intimidate me into doing anything of the sort. They could all go to hell as far as I was concerned. But if Scarborough was uncomfortable, then that was a completely different matter.

"Doesn't it bother you?" he asked.

"It's not likely that I'm ever going to see any of these people again, so they don't count for anything. The only person in this room who's important is the one in my arms right at this very minute." I continued moving, and Scarborough sighed and seemed to give up some of the tension in his body. That was amazing. The trust, the warmth, surrounded us, and I wanted the song to go on forever.

But all good things end, and the song and our dance were one of them. The music grew quieter and faded away. Scarborough straightened up and we separated. My heart beat like a bass drum and my body instantly missed the warmth and closeness. I took a single step away, and damned if Scarborough didn't smile at me.

"I think I need a drink," Scarborough said. "You?"

"A beer would be nice, and maybe some water." The last thing I wanted was to get tipsy. Judging from Scarborough's heady expression and half-lidded eyes, things might have changed between us. I still wasn't ready to let myself get truly excited. Scarborough could be a difficult one to read, and getting my hopes up was probably a recipe for disappointment.

I sat back at the table, and the others joined me. "My God, you two looked so cute together," Gwen said.

"Now, dear. They're friends," Buddy cautioned her. "Don't start seeing things just because you want them to be there." He patted her hand.

"A little romance and maybe a touch of fantasy never hurt anyone, and you saw them too. They were beautiful." Gwen leaned closer. "If you want my advice, strike while the iron is hot. He was so into you. You got the bait, and the line seems strong, so reel that puppy in." She winked, and I tried not to laugh as Scarborough set a beer and a glass of water on the table in front of me.

"Thanks," I said softly, and he sat down. The conversation around us continued, but Scarborough seemed mellow and kind of floaty as we sat there. He finished his beer, and I did the same, following it up with a glass of water.

AN HOUR or so later and after another glass of water, the party really began breaking up. Scarborough said goodbye to his friends with some bittersweet looks.

"Don't be a stranger," Buddy said, handing Scarborough a card. "Be sure to email or call. I don't want to wait for another of these to see you again." He hugged Scarborough and shook my hand. "I mean it."

"Okay," Scarborough agreed, and slipped the card into his pocket.

After a while of saying goodbyes, we left the hall. I took Scarborough's keys since I hadn't had much of anything to drink in nearly two hours, and got us back to the hotel. Scarborough was bouncy and all energy and smiles as we went up to our room. I had no idea what was going on in his head, but he made that clear as soon as the door closed and he pressed me back against it.

The energy that coursed through him was palpable, and I wound my arms around his waist, holding on while he took possession of my lips. There was no finesse in the kiss, but he more than made up for it with energy and sheer need. It was as enticing as anything I had ever experienced.

I was hard in seconds, holding Scarborough as he pushed closer, the wood of the door against my back, his legs shaking a little as he drew even nearer, hips pressing to mine. Damn, he was just as excited as I was, and I tightened my hold until his chest hugged mine. His breath tasted like beer and the mints from the table. I caressed his back and then up to his cheeks, drawing him nearer and taking charge of the kiss.

He groaned softly, and I pushed him back, guiding him through the room toward the bed. He held on to me as though I were a lifeline, and before there could be any more interruptions, my nimble fingers popped open button after button of Scarborough's shirt, exposing his smooth chest to my hands. God, I loved the chance to explore his body, and I did it with abandon, guiding him down onto the bed.

Scarborough seemed as anxious as I was, and it wasn't long before our clothes littered the floor. He lay on the bedcover, vibrating with excitement and anticipation, cock straining toward his belly button. God, he was stunning, and truthfully, I didn't know where to start with all of him laid out for me to explore.

I began with his legs, running my hands up his thighs to his hips and then up his belly, the hair on his legs tickling my hands.

"If you keep that up, I'm not going to last," Scarborough groaned. "Just touch me, please."

"Oh, I will." I climbed onto the bed, stalking up his body, my gaze locked on his. "You can count on it. But I want you to be good and ready." I leaned forward and sucked at the spot just above his belly button. God, Scarborough tasted good, and I continued prowling upward, lips blazing a trail up to his chest, muscles fluttering as I loved on them.

"Martin…," Scarborough begged.

I smiled, loving that sound as Scarborough bucked his hips lightly, becoming more desperate. "You're beautiful, you know that?" Scarborough had a typical cowboy tan, and I traced some of his tan lines. It seemed he rarely worked with his shirt off, as his arms and neck all had lines where his shirts fell.

"I am not. I'm just a cowboy farmer."

I paused. "And you think that isn't stunning? You are who you are, and that's enough. You don't need to be more or think there has to be something else in order for you to be desirable." I ran a finger down the cut in his belly. "You work hard, and it shows on your body." I kissed the center of his chest. "That's sexy."

Scarborough scoffed lightly. "Work is just work."

"No it's not. The life we lead leaves marks on us, both physically and otherwise. Your hard work has left its mark on your body." I captured his lips before he could argue with me again. I knew it wasn't exactly fair, but as I kept kissing, Scarborough's arms wound around my neck, and I pretty much figured he had forgotten what he wanted to say. Hell, I certainly had. My mind centered on each and every touch and sensation of Scarborough's body against mine.

The energy continued to build, and Scarborough's moans became more urgent by the second. I figured he needed some relief and grinned as I pulled away from his lips and slid down his body, running my tongue along him until my lips closed around the head of his cock. Damn, he tasted even better now, and Scarborough went nuts. It had clearly been quite some time since he'd been with anyone, and he groaned loudly, pressing upward, and I took him deep, bobbing my head a few times until he flooded my mouth with his release.

"Oh my God," Scarborough moaned softly as he collapsed back on the bedding. I chuckled and lay next to him, pulling him into my arms. "What about you?"

"It will wait a minute." Truthfully, I was thrilled with the glow that seemed to radiate off Scarborough. He was sexy, and the debauched smile on his lips was almost funny. In all the years I'd known Scarborough, I had never seen him looking so carefree and relaxed. He was always uptight and ready—and not the good kind. Like he expected the world to fall in on him at any second unless he was primed for action. This Scarborough was a whole new person, and I liked him even more.

Scarborough closed his eyes, and I smiled as his breathing evened out. I figured he must have had more beer than I thought, because within minutes he was asleep. I didn't wake him. Tomorrow was a busy day, and while we were here, everything was great, but I had no idea what the morning was going to bring.

CHAPTER 7

ALL MORNING and into the afternoon, Scarborough drove like a bat out of hell. That was the only description for it. He was lucky we didn't meet any police officers or he'd have gotten a ticket of epic proportions.

"Does everything look all right?" I asked after we'd pulled into his drive and had a chance to look around. I didn't see anything particularly out of place, but Scarborough seemed strung as tight as I had ever seen him. He stalked from stall to stall and then around the house.

"Sure. But I hate the idea that someone has been here, probably watching my home." He glanced from side to side. "What if they're watching us now?"

I looked around out of instinct and saw nothing. "I don't think that's the case." I tried to reassure him and patted his shoulder, but Scarborough moved away. That was not a good sign.

"It's just that this is my home," Scarborough explained. "This is supposed to be my safe place. It's mine and no one is going to take it from me, and they don't get to decide what happens here. I do." He turned to me with heat blazing in his eyes, but it wasn't the kind I would have hoped to see. Anger and frustration burned as hot as his passions last evening in the hotel.

"Then we need to find out what's going on and try to put an end to this. I think the best way is to find out where Storm came from." I wasn't sure how to do that, and the only link we had was through the auction house, and they weren't talking, at least not officially. A good share of their business was them accommodating the wishes of their clients, and they weren't going to give up information that their clients wished to be kept confidential. I was at a loss as to how to do what I was suggesting.

"I doubt we can," Scarborough said.

"Then what we need to do is be vigilant. If someone returns, we need to stop them and find out what they know and why they're here." I took a step closer. "I say we go Wild West on their asses. This is your property and your home, and they have no right to be snooping around. So we teach them some manners." I winked, and finally Scarborough smiled.

"We?" Scarborough asked. "Look, I can take care of things on my own place. I've been doing it for fifteen years, and I'm not going to change the way I do things now." The stubborn mule portion of his personality was definitely coming forward in spades.

"Yes, you have. But you have friends, and helping each other is what we do." I was getting a little tired of what felt like a merry-go-round. "Look, I know you seem to think that what happened last night was just something that took place because you were drunk and away from home." I took a deep breath and soldiered on, regardless of the hardness in Scarborough's eyes. "You can compartmentalize all you want, but I think the beer only let the feelings you've kept buried come forward." I crossed my arms and stared him down, daring him to tell me I was wrong.

"Maybe. But that doesn't change anything and it can't. I don't want to lose you as a friend, and—"

"So you consider pushing me away when I try to help you an endearing quality in a friend?" I rolled my eyes, and Scarborough sputtered. "Acting like an ass is suddenly your way of winning friends and influencing people? So you decide that since you don't want to deal… that somehow that's a bad thing." I could almost feel Scarborough's temper rising, and I waited for him to blow. But the hardness in his eyes subsided. I half expected to get punched, but instead he turned toward the house.

That was a reaction I hadn't anticipated, and I had no idea how to deal with it or what the fuck it meant. Just like with my father half the time, Scarborough had reverted into silence, and I wanted to scream about it. If he had yelled at me, I could deal with it…. Fuck, if he had lashed out, I could have done the same, and the two of us could have beaten the shit out of each other and then gone inside and fucked it out. I'd put up with a few bruises if it would help get past some of Scarborough's walls.

I thought about turning away and heading on home myself and letting Scarborough go back to the way things were, but that thought pissed me off. "You really are a piece of work, you know that?" I snapped.

He stopped and turned around. "I told you that when I got back home, I was going to have work to do…."

"Shit, Scarborough, so you got work to do. So do I. That doesn't mean you have to be an ass." Okay, maybe I was the one being an ass at the moment, but I was angry and fucking hurt. I deserved to be treated better than as a piece of meat.

He took a deep breath. "What do you want from me?"

"Maybe a little common decency. Let's try you letting me be your friend and you be mine." I slowly closed the gap between us, talking like I would to one of the horses. "How about you stop trying to push me and everyone else in town away, and you might be surprised at the number of people who would be willing to have your back."

Scarborough huffed and looked toward the house and then back at me, as though he were trying to make a decision but was being pulled apart. "You heard what my father wanted. I can't go through that again. Things here are settled for me. I can deal with them and lead a quiet life. That's all I really need. Can't you understand that?"

I shrugged because I couldn't really. "I guess I don't. I can't understand why you'll turn your back on something that has the chance to be pretty amazing out of fear. I never thought of you as being afraid."

Scarborough laughed, but it was filled with tension. "I spent the first part of my life working for my father and afraid each and every day. I had no idea when his temper would boil over or he would decide that I wasn't doing something right or he had changed his mind and wanted the nearly finished woodpile on the other side the barn. Yeah, he actually did that once because he's a complete and total shit. I can't have that in my life anymore."

"I'm not asking you to. I'm not your father, and I'm certainly not at all like him." I came even closer. "I'm your friend and the guy who got to see the real Scarborough under all these protective layers. And I'm not asking you to give them up. You were hurt, I get that, and I don't want you to let everyone waltz into your life and run roughshod over you. I'd be really angry and want to take them on if that happened. I'm just asking you to let me in. To lower those walls a little, or better yet, just build a doorway so I can get in." I backed away, figuring I had said more than enough. I wasn't going to get any answers or grand pronouncements out of Scarborough. I had said what I needed to, and now I figured it was time to go.

"I'll take you home," Scarborough said, and silently went to his truck.

I climbed in, and we rode to my house without saying a word. After unloading my things, I leaned on his window while he still had it open. "For now, I'll work with Storm at my dad's." I flashed a smile. "Call if you need anything." I backed away and hefted my gear, not turning around as I schlepped it all into the house.

Beau met me as soon as I came inside. Dad must have brought him back over. He yipped and jumped to get at me, bending himself into a half-moon around my legs so he could touch me as much as possible. "It's so good to see you too." I ruffled his coat and petted him, letting him know that I was back and had missed him.

My phone chimed with a message, but I finished saying hello to Beau and got him some treats before seeing who it was. I had hoped it was Scarborough, but instead it was Mom.

Come to dinner tonight.

I will, thanks, I sent back. After getting my laundry started, I put away my bag and the other things, including the huge stuffed dog that I had no idea what I was going to do with, as I carried it through the house trying to find a place for it. For now I set it in one of the living room chairs, because it still made me smile. "Wanna go check things out?" I asked Beau, who followed me outside, right on my heels, like I wasn't going anywhere without him.

The barn was clean and in good shape. Most of the horses were out in their paddocks, so I spot cleaned the stalls and checked on Dad's horse, moving him to finish my cleaning. I loved it when a barn smelled fresh, and after seeing that all the animals had food and water, inside and then outside, I gave them a treat as well. I was so happy to see each of them, and the horses—well, except for Dad's—came up to me for some attention. It was nice to be missed, and I stroked noses and patted necks, feeding them carrots.

Beau stayed right with me, and after a while, I tugged off my hat, wiped the sweat from my brow, and plunked it back down. Dang, it was hot. Each of the paddocks had a sheltered area, and the horses wandered away as I did, heading for the shade.

Inside, I caught up on my chores, took a shower, changed clothes. I took Beau with me out to the truck and headed to Mom and Dad's, where I found Mom in the kitchen. Dad was out and about, probably making some more deals.

"How was the trip?" Mom asked before turning around. She paused at the sink and smiled. "I see. It was a good one." I knew that "I told you so" smile. "Things were really good."

"Mom," I groaned, and turned away, pulling out a chair at the scarred wooden kitchen table.

"Well. You have that look, and don't tell me nothing happened. I know these things. I'm your mother." She turned back to the sink to finish the dishes. "Give me a minute, and I'll get us some iced tea and you can tell me what's bothering you." She rinsed the last of the dishes, put them in the rack, and drained the sink.

"He's… I don't know…. I guess I thought things would be different."

Mom actually snorted. "You figured you'd sleep with the guy and then everything would be hunky-dory and Scarborough would suddenly become the life of the party." She brought over the glasses and sat down.

"No. But I didn't think he'd turn his back either." God, I sounded whiny even to myself, and I hated it.

"I have news for you. The penis isn't a cure-all." She smirked, and I groaned, unable to believe my mother was saying these things. "Well…." She sipped her tea. "You slept with him, and then you expected everything to be fine. He would follow you around like Beau, and he'd change his entire outlook on life and become the perfect person for you." She lightly whapped me on the side of the head.

"Geez, Mom."

"Then don't be stupid. Scarborough is the man he is, and you have to let him be. That's part of loving someone. He isn't going to suddenly turn into a party animal. And that's a good thing, because you already know him and care for him as he is. That's special."

I leaned forward. "But you should have seen him. At the reunion he talked with people for hours while I spent a lot of time sitting at the table. He even danced with me when the ladies formed a shield. Mom, it was amazing. I got to dance with him. It was like he had become someone so different, and I liked that person a lot. Not that I don't like the person he is here, but he's so closed off, and those walls he's built around himself are like they're loaded with land mines and thorns." At least now I had a pretty good idea why, but I kept that information to myself. It had been shared in confidence, and I wasn't going to break it. Not even with Mom.

"Then it is the way it is." She sipped some more, and I did the same because I wasn't sure what else to do as Mom seemed to gather her thoughts. "You need to give Scarborough the chance to figure out what he wants. Did he have a good time?"

"He did until Dad said he thought people had been on the ranch. Then he came home driving like a madman. I spent hours holding on for dear life." I flashed a grin. "But yeah, he had a good time and he smiled... a lot." I wanted to see him smile that way much more often.

Mom patted my hand. "You need to give him a chance to figure some things out. He may have viewed the trip with you as just a chance to let his hair down. He could be the way he wanted because there were no consequences to it. He was on vacation, and now he's returned to real life. I don't really know what he's thinking. None of us will." She flashed another of those smiles. "That's the fun part. You get to try to discover it, and you have to look for clues. Lord knows I had to with your father, to a degree. But if you want my advice, give him a little time... but not too much time. And if necessary, be persistent."

"I will, Mom."

"Oh, and find out who hurt that beautiful horse so I can hunt them down and cut their nuts off. Whoever did that committed a crime against nature, and they deserve to pay for it." She set her glass on the table and pushed back her chair.

"I'll try, Mom. I told Scarborough that I was going to train Storm here, but I think I'm going to ask Dad to help me move him back to Scarborough's. He needs to be in his own environment." I smiled because it would give me an excuse to be at Scarborough's and see him without appearing to get in his business.

Mom smiled. "Now you're thinking." She took her glass to the sink, and I got up as well. I had plenty of work to do and needed to get started. After thanking Mom for the tea, I headed out to the barn to check on Storm and get my plans to visit a client in order before dinner.

THE FOLLOWING morning, I walked Storm into Scarborough's barn. Dad had already arranged to take his horse home, and I slipped Storm into the paddock. He seemed like such a different horse than the one I'd first met. He was almost docile and didn't seem bothered by me or my proximity in the least. Still, I hadn't wanted to move him in a trailer, and walking him home seemed like good exercise for both of us, even if it took a while and was hot as billy hell.

"Your wayward boy is back home," I told Scarborough as I closed the gate. "He did really well." As soon as he was alone in the paddock, Storm raced around the perimeter, seemingly checking things out, and then settled once again, but he didn't start eating. Instead, he seemed to watch me without getting closer.

"Maybe I just bought a horse that's crazy." Scarborough leaned on the fence rail as Storm began to eat. "I don't get it at all."

"I think part of what we've been seeing is conditioning," I told him. "The snakes and things. That horse has had something traumatic done to him with snakes." The more I talked about it, the more the idea solidified.

"But why would someone want to do that, and why come here?"

I nodded and turned to him. "It's something Iris said at the reunion. Maybe he was used for testing of some sort, and maybe he was sent to auction by mistake."

"That sounds like grasping at straws," Scarborough said as his gaze met mine. I tried not to react to it, but damn, the air around me grew ten degrees warmer, I swear.

"No. That's just thinking. The straws are yet to come." I flashed him a smile. "So if he was sold too early, they still needed something from him. They came here and put the snakes in his paddock to see how he reacted. Then they returned to watch him as he calmed down with no further adverse stimulation. Maybe they were giving him some drugs or something, and they've been working out of his system. I'm not really sure." Even what I was saying sounded a little nuts, but it sort of fit what we had been seeing. Maybe some part of it reflected reality.

"Okay. So what sort of people test stuff like that on horses? They're big animals and expensive to keep," Scarborough asked, and I shrugged. "No university is going to do it. Sounds way too unethical to me."

"The military?" I offered, and he rolled his eyes. "Government, maybe something they sponsored?" It was sounding even more far-fetched by the minute. "Okay, that's sounding really stupid, even to me, and I was the one who came up with the whole thing. If someone shows up again, we need to catch them and find out what the hell is going on."

"Agreed," Scarborough said, to my surprise. I had expected resistance. "If anyone shows, I'll call you for backup and—"

"They'll be long gone before I can get here. You know that. As soon as anyone sees any activity, they'll take off quick. We need to keep Storm safe, and we need to watch him."

"What are you suggesting? I'm not moving to your place, and you don't need to stay here. You're a mile up the road, and it will take you two minutes to get here. I can take care of my own place." His expression softened. "But I appreciate the backup. I really do." He sighed. "I need a chance to work everything through, okay?"

"Sure." At least he was thinking about what happened between us and not just sloughing it off.

"Come over when you can to work with Storm, and I'll figure my shit out. I promise."

"Okay." I checked the time and realized I had to get back home and out to a client's or I was going to be late. I said goodbye and headed across the field, with Beau right next to me, checking where I was every few minutes, tongue hanging out. I hated to admit it, but it bothered me to leave things unresolved. I'd probably gotten as much from Scarborough as I was going to, and what he'd asked for wasn't unreasonable. It was time to get back to work and for real life to begin once again. "Come on, Beau." I took off, and he raced next to me. Maybe getting my blood pumping would get this unsettled feeling out of my head.

CHAPTER 8

STORM WAS behaving well. He was still a little skittish at times, but when I showed up to work with him, he actually approached to get his treat, ears perking as I spoke to him softly. In a few weeks, it might be possible to put a saddle on him. If we could get to the point where he would trust us enough to do that, I figured my job was done. He wasn't going to be a good riding horse, but by that time, with his conformation, he'd be good for breeding.

"He's surprisingly calm," Scarborough said from nearby. Storm turned toward him, watching and listening.

"Something was definitely off when you brought him here. Part of it could be the quiet and the fact that he's starting to feel safe, but I don't know." Everything about the situation with Storm had me confused. I had honestly expected to spend months getting this horse to trust me and stop trying to kill everyone around him. "He was well trained once, and maybe it's that training that's coming through." I patted his neck and fed him another treat before continuing to work with him. Mostly I talked and got him used to being around me, hoping he would remain calm. Eventually I released him from the lead and backed away. I didn't trust him enough to turn my back. Storm stood still, and then I reached the gate. It squeaked as I opened it, and Storm took off toward the back of the paddock, not stopping until he was as far away as possible.

"I didn't see that coming," Scarborough said, and I shook my head.

"He was trained, and someone really messed him up pretty badly." I closed the gate and stood at the fence, watching Storm. He snorted and breathed heavily, head bobbing, stamping the ground. We waited and eventually Storm calmed down, but it took a while. "If he had scars, I'd know why."

"That doesn't mean he wasn't beaten," Scarborough said. "I've been giving it some thought. If he did something wrong and he was beaten or mistreated by someone, we'd get this kind of behavior. Think about it—maybe the sound of the gate is a trigger, like some sort of PTSD for horses. I read once that horses used in war were often shell-shocked and that they would get unfit for use because the noise would get to them. I mean, in the movies the horses never react until they're at the critical moment." He backed away. "Let's leave him alone for a while, and I'm going to oil that gate."

I wasn't going to argue on that point. "Look, Scarborough… I…." I had been wondering how to broach the subject of what had happened between us in Nebraska, and I wasn't sure. He seemed content not to talk about it, and maybe that was best. Maybe he and I should just go back to being friends, but I kept seeing his face at night and thinking of how he felt sleeping next to me. I wanted that again. "There's a party in town on Saturday. It's the annual Red Rock Summer Festival. Mom and Dad are going, and I wondered if you wanted to go."

"So people can point and talk about me behind my back?" He scowled.

"No. You can go with us and have a good time," I countered. "It's always fun, and there are games and things. Nothing like the carnival, but the local civic clubs make food and sponsor activities and games. It helps fund some of the activities at the school." I wasn't holding out much hope, but I thought if I could tap into some of the fun we had in Nebraska, I might convince him. "They're looking for donations and help…." I waited.

Scarborough nodded. "I could give them the big dog I won. It isn't like I need it in the house."

I smiled. I had been thinking the same thing. "So you'll come with us?"

His shoulders slumped a little, but then he stood straighter. "I'll go. How bad could it be?"

I rolled my eyes. "Good God. If you really think it's going to be like getting dental work done, then you shouldn't come. This is a fun time, and the town all gets together to support the school and help pay for additional things. There's a three-on-three basketball tournament and a home-run contest. Those support the sports program, but the rest of the fair supports the art and music programs. We all want our kids to have the best chance they can."

Scarborough smiled. "Okay. It sounds like it could be fun."

"Then I'll pick you up on Saturday and we can have dinner at the fair. The school boosters have a fried chicken stand that is out of this world. The leader of the boosters moved here with her husband years ago from Alabama, and she knows her chicken. It's her recipe, and they make it just like they do in the South." My stomach was already growling. That was one of the highlights of the food year for me.

"Okay, you convinced me," Scarborough said, this time with a genuine smile. Damn, Mom was right—maybe I could thaw Scarborough's chill with food. "I'll see you Saturday." He pushed away from the fence. "Now I have things to do, and I suspect you do too." Scarborough headed toward the barn and then stopped. "Do you want to come to dinner on Thursday? I don't cook a lot, but I can probably put something together."

My legs nearly gave out in shock. In fifteen years, I had never been invited to dinner at Scarborough's. In fact, I had only been inside on a few occasions. We usually met out in the yard and talked things over there. I guess you could say up until now that ours had been largely an outdoor friendship.

"That would be great." I smiled, and he continued on his way. "Come on, Beau, we have places to be." We hopped into the truck, stopped at the house for a quick check of the barn, then headed off to my next client on the other side of the county to work with a horse who needed rehabilitation after some surgery.

THURSDAY COULDN'T come fast enough for me. I slept with the phone next to the bed in case Scarborough called, but everything was quiet on that front. I did notice that Scarborough had more lights on outside than usual when I passed on my way home in the evenings. When I was in town, I stopped at the store and bought a couple of interesting six-packs to take with me to dinner. I wasn't sure what he was serving, but beer went with most things, and Scarborough had seemed to like it at the reunion.

"No, Beau. You stay here and guard the house."

He wanted to go badly, but at my tone, sat by the door with those huge "don't leave me" eyes. It was nearly enough to make me change my mind, but I told him to stay, and he slunk over, jumped on the couch, and lay down while still fixing me with that gaze.

"I'm not leaving you forever, just for the evening."

He blinked and went back to that look.

I left the house before I gave in, putting my kit in the truck just in case. I was such a softie, but I wasn't looking forward to getting hair all over my clothes. I'd worn jeans and a new shirt. I also had on the new pair of boots I'd gotten a few weeks ago and needed to break in.

When I got to Scarborough's, the place was lit up like a church. I wondered if something had happened, but he came out on the porch and waved. I approached him, and damned if he didn't look good. His jeans were tight, and he had on a green polo that hugged his arms and chest just right.

"Trying to deter any unwanted visitors."

"I hope you got good curtains in your room," I teased, and he nodded, opening the door, and I went inside with the beer, placing my kit on the table near the door.

Scarborough's place was immaculately clean, if a little sparse. The wood floors shone, and the sofa had a dark blue slipcover. The chairs were soft, worn leather and had probably been there for nearly the entire time he'd lived here. The few pictures hanging on the wall were horses, probably images taken right outside. It was most definitely a cowboy kind of place—comfortable without being frilly.

"Do you want to put these in the refrigerator? I thought you might like them based on what you were drinking when you were home." I handed him the cold six-packs, and he took them into the other room, then returned with two bottles.

"I don't have many guests, so... I'm not like your mom. I don't really know what to do. I got some cheese and crackers and stuff at the store." He hurried away, and I realized he was nervous. When he returned, he set a plate on the table, the cheese squares and crackers ringing the edge of the plate like they had been perfectly shuffled and arranged, with a few additional crackers in the center. It was so nice and just another sign of how nervous he was.

"Just relax. You can't really do anything wrong unless you forgot the food. And if that happened, then we just go to town." I shrugged and sat on the sofa, opening my beer.

Scarborough seemed to hover and then sat down in one of the chairs, which creaked softly under his weight. He sipped from his beer and generally stared at the ceiling. It was almost painful to watch him.

"How did you end up coming to Red Rock?" I asked, and some of the tension eased for him.

"I had been working all over this area for a while. I didn't want to work in Nebraska. So Wyoming became the next choice. And I came here a few times as a child." He screwed up his face in a way that left me with the impression that he was trying to remember something just out of reach. "We never took vacations, but Dad brought me here with Mom." He smiled and nodded. "He said he had some important meetings or something. Mom stayed with me at the room he'd rented. They didn't talk about why we were here, but Mom took me to the park, and I remember having fun while I was here. Maybe because Dad was busy, Mom and I got to play a little." His face lost some of the hard edges it usually had. "I worked and saved, and I saw an ad in a real estate magazine for the land here. And I remembered the fun I'd had and thought this might be a good place." He shrugged again, and I wondered just how precious those memories were to him. "The house was run down, and so were the rest of the buildings… as you probably know after helping me rebuild the barn and stuff. But I was able to afford it and some initial livestock. There were two horses already here that the previous owner had just left outside to fend for themselves. I got them inside and cared for and eventually sold them to make some more money and buy some of the kind of stock I really wanted. From there I sort of built the ranch up with a lot of hard work."

I leaned forward a little. "Why didn't you try to become part of the town and get to know people? You had to know that not everyone here was going to be like your dad. And you had good memories of this place. It was your chance to start over and maybe have the life you wanted." God, at least it looked that way to me, but then, I hadn't been through all the things that Scarborough had. So maybe he simply needed a place he thought of as safe. I had to remind myself that not everyone needed the same things.

"I met your mom and dad right away, and they were really nice. But…." He took a long drink of beer. "I was damaged. I think I still am. And afraid. If I relied on others and then they took that away…." He sighed. "It was just easier and safer to do things on my own. I grew the ranch to the point where it sustains itself and me. I can handle it, so that's what I do. I have savings in case something happens, and from there I basically do what I want. I don't need the help of the town, and I sell most of my beef to one of the local markets. It's high quality, and they have their own butcher department, so they're thrilled to get it, and I get a better price than most people. I don't use chemicals anywhere on the ranch, and the cattle eat only grass that I grow myself. I'm working on an organic certification, and once that comes through, I'll be able to charge even more."

"Wow." I'd had no idea and was damned impressed. "That must take a while."

"It does, but I'm a good way through it and should get there pretty soon. That alone will mean a lot to me. I'm really careful to buy my calves from other organic ranches, and I breed some of my own." He sat back and sipped some more. "I really like it here, and I've built my place into something I can be proud of."

"That's impressive." And it was. I'd had no idea he was going for the whole organic thing and—

A horse screamed outside, pulling my attention. I set the beer on the table and went to the door. Scarborough jumped up, and we both hurried out into the twilight in time to see someone moving in Storm's paddock. The horse was as far away as he could get. Scarborough had grabbed a rifle and raced around me.

"What the hell do you think you're doing there?" Scarborough yelled, raising the gun, and I thought he was going to shoot the guy right there.

"Nothing," the figure said shakily, and backed away from the horse and toward the gate.

"Get out of there," Scarborough said, and held the gun steady as the young man closed the gate and slowly turned around.

"Clint?" I asked, recognizing the kid. "Answer him!" I stepped closer, and Scarborough lowered the gun. "Your mother is going to skin you alive when she finds out what you're doing, and your dad….” All I had to do was mention both of them, and Clint began to shake.

Scarborough turned to me, quizzically. “Who is this?”

“One of the kids from town,” I answered, stepping forward and grabbing Clint’s arm. “Now, I think you owe us an explanation for what you’re doing here.”

“I can’t tell you,” Clint said. “They won’t let me in if I do.”

I pulled him toward the porch. “Fine. You can sit on the porch while I call your parents, and they can deal with you.” I checked my watch. “Your dad ought to be at home having dinner, or is he up at the hospital visiting the sick?” I crossed my arms over my chest and glared at him. “Or I could call my mother.” That was one hell of a threat, and he knew it. Mom was a fixture in the church and all the kids liked her, so to have her upset with you was something pretty bad.

“I can’t tell. They’ll never let me in otherwise,” he said, pushing out his lower lip.

I nodded. “You don’t need to tell me. I had a friend who tried to get in the club when I was your age. He had to tip one of Mr. Harrington’s cows in order to get in.” I shook my head. It had been stupid then and it still was.

“So you do understand. I want to be part of the Skull and Dagger Club.”

That was too damned easy. I glared at him, and Clint groaned.

“What the hell is the Skull and Dagger Club?” Scarborough asked.

“It’s one of those ‘secret’ clubs at St. Alban’s military school.” I rolled my eyes. “They have been hazing their members with some sort of stupid initiation for years.” I turned to Clint. “I’ll let you in on a secret. If they sent you out here to do something to one of Scarborough’s horses, they don’t want you in the club. They sent you out here to get in trouble so you’d leave them alone.” My God, was this the source of the shit going on?

"But they said if I…." He seemed confused and unsure of himself now.

"I think you need to come to the porch and tell us everything that's been happening." About this time, I figured Clint was catching on to the trick I had pulled on him. "You aren't going to help yourself by staying quiet. The only one who will get hurt now is you. The police will come, and they are going to have plenty of questions. I'll call your father, and you know he isn't going to be nice."

Clint began to shake. "But they said… I didn't hurt anything." He sputtered. "And I'd never hurt a horse. I just needed to get a hair from his tail. That was all."

"Storm would kick your head in before you got close to him, kid. Did you see how he was acting?" Scarborough asked, and met my gaze. "I'm going to call the police. Let him tell them all his excuses."

I guided Clint onto the porch and sat him in one of the chairs. "Let's see what he has to say for himself." I thought Clint was seconds from wetting himself. His bravado, what little he'd had, was gone, and his eyes were huge and filled with fear.

"I was just supposed to get a hair from him. Nothing more. I wasn't going to let him go or nothing." He shook, and I sat back to let him talk, sharing a brief glance with Scarborough. "I wanted to join the club. It's the one all the cool kids are part of, and I'm tired of being on the outside of everything. My dad's a preacher, so everyone expects me to be a Goody Two-shoes or something." He took a deep breath. "I wanted to be interesting and popular for once in my life." He sniffled. "One of the other guys got in here and said it was easy. He put fake snakes in the paddock and took pictures of the horse and stuff. They let him in, and all they said I had to do was get a hair from the same horse. They said it was wild, but when I got here, I couldn't find it. I thought it was in the barn, but I didn't see it. Then it was out in the paddock again, and….." He put his hand over his face. "I'm never gonna get into anything fun."

I had heard just about enough. "You could have gotten killed and hurt Storm in the process. And did your friends tell you that they put a live snake in the paddock? They didn't care if the horse got killed or if one of us did." I was angry as hell. "That horse could have broken a leg or worse, and all you and your friends were worried about was joining some stupid club at school." I wasn't sure what the fuck I wanted to do and sat back, clenching my hands. Whatever happened next was up to Scarborough.

"I didn't know that, and I wasn't part of it, I swear. I would never put a snake in a horse's paddock. That's just mean." He paled, and I had a pretty good idea he was telling the truth.

I lifted my gaze to Scarborough. "What do you want to do? He was on your land, and he was in the paddock with Storm." This was his decision.

"You are going to tell us all about this club," Scarborough said. "And then you're going to call your parents and have them come out here to get you." He sighed. "Now start talking or the call I make will be to the police, and they can deal with you and your club friends." He scowled, though I was pretty sure it was a put-up job.

"I don't know that much. It's the cool kids, and they get to meet in a special room at the school." He began coughing and tugged out an inhaler, took a pull, and held it in his lungs before slowly releasing his breath. "The people in charge and the headmaster were all members of the club once, and now they oversee it and stuff." He took a careful breath. "I just wanted to be part of something."

"By giving up an important part of who you are," Scarborough said. "Those club people don't care about anyone other than themselves. They could have gotten you seriously injured or hurt

Storm, all over some stupid club initiation and getting other people to do the stupid things they wanted them to do."

Scarborough stood, left the porch, and went out to Storm's paddock. He checked the fence, came back with a few long hairs, and handed them to Clint. "If this is so important to you, then take them. But remember what you're selling yourself short for. Just getting into a club isn't going to make you popular." He went inside, the screen door slamming closed behind him.

"Is that it?" Clint asked.

I shrugged. "I think he's telling you that you have to decide what kind of man you want to be. He gave you what you wanted, and you could take that back to your club and maybe they would let you in. But is that what you really want? Is a club worth the things they tried to get you to do? And what if they decide you have to do something worse? That this is just the first step. Are you going to do that?" I sat back and waited.

Clint stood, slowly descended the steps of the porch, and headed down the driveway with his prize.

I waited until he was gone and then went inside, finding Scarborough in the kitchen.

"Stupid kids. They'll do the stupidest things to get into some club or be accepted by people who aren't ever going to have anything to do with them." He chopped potatoes with enough force that he was going to cut straight through the board. "How old is he, fifteen?"

"I think sixteen, and you know how it is at that age. Kids just want to belong and not be on the outside looking in." God, I remembered how that felt.

"Were you on the outside?"

"Not really. I had a group of friends. I was in junior rodeo, which gave me people who liked the same things I did. What about you?"

Scarborough snorted. "I guess I thought I wasn't very popular, but I think that was just how I looked at things. I think

I had some good friends, and that made school bearable." He finished the potatoes and put them in a pot of water on the stove. "I hope he figures things out." Scarborough pulled out the steaks from the refrigerator and began seasoning them. "These came from my herd. I grow as much of my own food as I can. I have a freezer full of beef and pork, and I have a big garden. I grow a lot of vegetables and some of my own fruit." He motioned out back behind the house, where the land was laid with a patchwork of rows and mounds. "It's nothing fancy, but I have three freezers in the cellar, and I fill one with meat and one with vegetables. The other is general storage, and then I have a pantry with things I can and preserve."

"I thought you said you didn't cook."

"Just simple stuff. It's only for me, so I don't often make big meals. But what I have is enough to get me through, and then I hunt in the fall and butcher and skin my own catch. That gets frozen too, and I make some of it into sausage." He pulled a salad out of the refrigerator, and it looked to me like he and I were having a feast. "I'm going to put the steaks on." He left me standing there to watch over what he had on the stove. Sometimes I wondered if I was ever going to understand Scarborough. Maybe that was the attraction. That man would always keep me guessing and on my toes.

I tended the potatoes and waited for him to come back inside. He checked them with a fork and then set me to mashing them while he finished up with the steak. That was something I could do, and after adding a little milk and a dollop of sour cream and some butter, I put them in the bowl Scarborough had set out, just about the time he came back inside with the steaks on a plate.

"What are you really going to do about Clint?"

"Nothing for now. Though I am going to have a word with the headmaster at that school and tell him that I will hold him personally responsible for any damage his students cause. What they're doing isn't right."

"I can speak to the sheriff," I offered. "He and my dad have known each other for a long time."

"Thanks. I want this to stop. I shouldn't have to worry about my property like this." He set the platter on the table, and I brought over the potatoes and salad. Scarborough got a clear glass container of dressing.

"What is that?"

Scarborough shrugged. "I was hungry for some of the things that my mom used to make, so I found a recipe for herb vinaigrette on the internet. It turned out pretty well, and the herbs came from the garden, so they're fresh." He set it on the table, and I sat down.

"Okay. I'm going to say it again: you can cook pretty well." Why he thought this wasn't impressive was beyond me. It showed a great deal of care and planning.

Scarborough reached back and pulled open the pantry door. "Usually I make something and have soup to go with it."

I peered inside and boggled at what had to be nearly two hundred cans of soups of all different kinds.

"I didn't think you wanted canned soup for dinner, so I tried to come up with something nicer that I could make. If you come to dinner again, you'll probably get the same meal or chicken with stars soup."

I smiled. "If I get to have dinner and spend time with you, then chicken and noodles soup from a can will be just fine. It's the company that makes a meal special." Oh, and that steak. It was seasoned amazingly and melted in the mouth. Jesus, this had to be one of the best pieces of beef I had ever eaten. Dad raised amazing beef, but holy cow. I barely stopped to eat anything else as I plowed through the steak, bite after incredible bite.

"Good?"

I shook my head. "Stellar. You need to sell this to people, and not at the grocery store. This needs to be sold with your name on it. People will pay a lot for meat that tastes like this." It was sublime. The fat was perfectly marbled and carried the flavor of the seasonings.

"You think so?"

I nodded. "Hell yes. Those Omaha Steak people have nothing on this." I continued eating and then tried the salad. Man, that was good. Fresh lettuce, the dressing perfect with the vegetables. God, each bite seemed better than the last one.

By the time we'd finished eating, I felt like a tick about to pop. Everything had been amazing, and apparently Scarborough had fresh ice cream in the freezer, not that I could eat a bite, at least not right away. He and I returned to the living room and sat side by side on the sofa, feet up on the table, a pleasant food coma overtaking both of us.

I sighed. "That was so good." Closing my eyes, I let the quiet work its way inside. Living out here away from town and most people, I understood the joy of silence.

"Thanks." He didn't say more, and we sat still. Eventually I turned my head to look. Scarborough laid out long and calm was a beautiful thing. I simply watched him and didn't move otherwise. There was no rush, and sitting together without a bunch of conversation was fine and not at all uncomfortable. "Why are you smiling?"

"Because my mother would have filled the silence with a mile of chatter on just about any subject she could think of, just to fill the space." I smiled, and without thinking, took Scarborough's hand in mine. I didn't make a big deal of it and just sat there.

"Do you want a beer?" Scarborough asked after a while and then got up. I nodded, and he left and returned with two open bottles. I wondered if I'd moved too fast, but he sat back down and took my hand once again. It was nice, and I smiled before taking a sip from the bottle. "You were right," Scarborough said, breaking the quiet that had settled around us once again.

"I like being right, but you're going to have to give me a little more." I winked at him.

"Things can't go back to the way they were before. It just isn't going to work that way." Scarborough squeezed my hand. "You made me want things…." He stammered a little. "I was fine before, and I had a life that I could understand and control, and then…." He let go of my hand and stood. "Now after being with you… I want more of that, and it scares the shit out of me." He began pacing a little like the way Beau did when a storm was brewing. "You spoiled me."

"And maybe you deserve to be spoiled," I told him. "And maybe it should happen often and with as much regularity as possible." I stood and set my bottle on the coffee table.

"I don't know how to act sometimes when it comes to things like this. It's not something I'm good at. I can raise beef and handle horses and grow things, but when it comes to other people, I figured for a long time that I was better off staying away." He seemed so lost, and that look in his eyes was the same one Beau had when I'd left him back at the house.

I wrapped my arms around Scarborough and tugged him closer. "Do you remember that night in the hotel?" I asked quietly, and he nodded, licking his lips. "Remember what it felt like in bed with me right next to you, and you…?" I leaned closer, sucking at the base of his ear. I had learned a few things that night, and damned if Scarborough didn't moan softly. I hugged him tighter, and he fit, like he was made for me to hold. "Remember when I kissed you…?" I added, his breath tickling my lips as I drew nearer.

A knock left me groaning, and two seconds later, Scarborough's phone rang. The fucking place had suddenly turned into Grand Central Station. I pulled back. "I'll get the door while you answer the phone." I turned away and swore under my breath. I hadn't even gotten to kiss him, and I'd been wanting a refresher course in the flavor of his lips for days.

"Clint," I said after opening the door.

He thrust his fist toward me with the long strands of black hair still in his fingers. "They didn't believe me and said that I didn't get in, and then they gave me something else to do, just like you guys said they would." He dropped the hair. "Fuck them all." He turned and stalked down the stairs.

"Clint," I said gently. He was sixteen years old and trying to figure things out. I knew what that felt like.

I motioned to Clint to come back, and then went inside, and Scarborough was just in the kitchen, standing in the doorway, looking about as tense as I could ever remember him being. Then he jabbed the phone and tossed it into the chair. With the way he seemed, I wouldn't have been surprised if he threw it across the room.

"Do you want something to drink?" I asked Scarborough, who came up behind me.

"No good?" Scarborough asked, and Clint's shoulders sank. The kid looked defeated. "Have a seat and I'll get you a Coke." He went back toward the kitchen, and Clint came inside. I closed the door and took a seat on the sofa, putting my feet up. Scarborough returned and sat next to me, with Clint in the chair across from us. He looked a little like he was in the hot seat. "Relax, kid, and tell us what happened."

Clint opened the can and drank, burped, and then set it down. "I told them I had done what they wanted, and they said that it wasn't enough and that I needed to come back and ride the horse. Then they all laughed and just left. Like I was nothing. The jackasses."

"No one can ride that horse. Not now and maybe not ever," I explained softly. "He's been hurt, and he doesn't trust anyone other than me a little and Scarborough." Maybe my dad too, but I wasn't going to make a fucking list. "What did you do?"

"I told them to go fuck themselves, and the headmaster was there, and he gave me detention for swearing." He huffed, and I shared a look with Scarborough.

"It seems the headmaster there is part of the problem." What kind of man promoted this sort of thing? It made no sense to me. This was supposed to be a military academy teaching discipline, not encouraging their students to run wild and put each other in danger.

"The senior boys all kind of run the school in a way." He looked down at his shoes. "Now the bigger kids will—" He snapped his mouth shut.

"You get bullied, don't you?" I asked. Clint wasn't a big guy by any means, and he had always seemed so eager to please. Almost too much so, and I was willing to bet the boys pounced on that and left him the butt of their jokes.

"Sometimes, I guess. I asked my dad to let me go to public school, but he said that St. Albans would be good for me and make me a man. That it would toughen me up. My sisters get to go to regular school, but I have to go to St. Assface." He drank some more of his soda and then stood. "I'm sorry I bothered you. I should get back home. Dad will be wondering where I am, and if I'm not there by curfew, he'll be mad." Clint left, and I waited until he walked away and out of the drive.

"Isn't it summer? Why is all this happening now? School shouldn't be in session." Scarborough seemed genuinely confused, and I couldn't blame him.

I sighed. "They have summer terms there, and the clubs and groups have meetings sometimes. They also pick their new members during the summer, which explains why we're having some trouble. If the damned club has decided that you're some sort of initiation, then this shit is going to continue until we put a stop to it." I took his hand.

"I can handle it," Scarborough said.

"No. *We* can handle it. The headmaster of St. Assface—" I actually had to laugh at the name. "—has quite a reputation. And remember that he's involved with the club. You and I will go and put up a united front. The bigger the offense, the better our chance of making an impact."

Scarborough shrugged. "If you really think it's necessary. The man is an educator—he should know better than to put his students in danger and to encourage them to commit a crime."

"Who really knows what's going on there? Sometimes schools and institutions like that have developed a culture and tradition that have their own rules, and they don't think of the consequences." I was more curious about having a talk with the reverend about his son, but I doubted the man was going to listen to me. Clint's father wasn't known for being accepting of the opinions of others. He knew what he knew, and his opinions were pretty much fact and law as far as I could see. Clint had a long row to hoe with his dad if he was going to convince him to put him in public school. I felt for the kid, I really did.

I purposely didn't ask about the call Scarborough had received. He still seemed on edge, and I hated whoever had called to make him that way. I leaned closer, and to my surprise he rested against me. I wasn't going to push for anything more, but it was nice that Scarborough seemed affectionate.

"The call was my dad," Scarborough said after a while. "He says he has to come over to Wyoming and wants to see me."

I was shocked, to say the least. "He didn't see you when we were in Nebraska and asked you for money, and now he's going to be here and wants to see you? I don't get it."

"He wants money and is going to put the moves on me. I'm sure of it. Somehow he thinks seeing him is going to change my mind." Scarborough seemed to tense. "Though he said he got a loan, so…." He huffed softly. "I don't know. I wish he would stay away. I told him there was a small hotel in Red Rock. I wasn't going to have him staying here with me."

"Good for you." Scarborough had said that this was his safe place more than once, so it made sense to me that he'd want to keep his father away.

"Apparently he's on his way to the area for some sort of supplier meeting or something. I think it's the same kind of meeting that we first traveled here for when I was a kid." Scarborough was still tense as hell. "I don't want to see him. This is my town now, and I don't want him to color it for me." He turned on the sofa to face me. "I could tell him not to come, but it seems cowardly. He is my father, and even if I don't like him, he's still my dad and he is coming all this way. I can see him and see what he has to say."

I shrugged. "Maybe he sees that he treated you badly and wants to make things right," I offered.

"And the moon is made of green cheese." Scarborough's slight laugh broke some of the tension. "Whatever it is, I didn't mean for him to put a damper on the evening." He left and returned with a couple more beers. "I have to go check on things for the night. You can wait here if you like, or…."

I took the beer and stood, stepping right in front of him. "What is it you want, Scarborough? I can go home if you need to work and then go to bed… or I can wait for you to come back." I placed my hand on his chest. "It's up to you." Just being close to him was enough to raise the temperature in the room, and damn it all, I wanted him. I had all evening. Every time he touched my hand, I wanted to pull him into a kiss that would melt the furniture. But I had held back to give him space. He seemed almost flustered, and I wanted to put it out there and let him decide what he wanted.

He licked his lips, and his eyes widened a little. "I just need to check that everything is okay and that the place is buttoned up."

"Do you want me to come?" I asked.

Scarborough handed me the television remote. "Relax a few minutes. This isn't going to take long." He pointed to the cabinet.

"There are some movies down in the cabinet if you want to watch one. I'll be half an hour." He hurried out to the barn and disappeared inside.

I stood to watch him through the front window, wondering if I was ever going to understand him fully.

I checked the radar on my phone and followed him out. "Scarborough," I called as I neared the barn. "It looks like a storm is heading our way." Usually in late summer we were lucky to get rain once a week, but it seemed we were in some sort of storm track. "I need to go home myself and make sure everything is closed up." I approached where he was pulling open the side doors to bring in the horses.

"I smelled it on the air. You do what you need to." He paused and turned to me.

I drew closer, tugged him into my arms, and kissed him hard. "It isn't going to be too bad, but I left the horses out and I'd rather they were inside. I'll hurry home and come back… if you want me to."

Scarborough nodded. "I want you to."

I kissed him again. "Then I won't be too long." I turned and headed away. "I need to feed Beau as well."

"Bring him. He'll be fine, and I know he hated that you were away." He went back to work as a rumble sounded in the distance.

I raced to the truck and down the road, pulled into the yard, and ran to the barn. The horses were near the doors, so it was easy getting them inside and bedded down for the night. Lightning lit the sky as I closed the door and opened the one to the house, calling for Beau. He raced out, watered the grass, and then jumped into the truck when I held the door. I got inside and yanked it closed as the first drops hit the windshield.

The sky opened up as I turned on the road, and I could barely see as I slowly drove the familiar distance to Scarborough's. I drove in and right up the house. He'd left the lights on or I wouldn't have known where the house was, it was raining so hard. Not that I was going to complain. We needed any liquid sunshine we could get, and the entire area was going to breathe a sigh of drought relief at a second rain in a week. "Come on, Beau, we're going to need to make a run for it." I got out and hurried to the porch. Beau made it first and he was soaked, his hair matted to his skin. He shook, sending the water that I hadn't managed to collect all over me.

Scarborough brought some towels as the rain let up, settling into something gentler. I tugged off my shirt and let it fall to the floor on the porch and then took off my boots. Scarborough handed me a towel and started rubbing down Beau, though he seemed to be paying more attention to me than he was to him. "Umm, you should go on inside. I can put your shirt and stuff in the dryer."

Beau pulled away and went right inside. Thankfully he was good enough that he sat on the floor and didn't try to jump on the furniture when he was wet. I followed Scarborough into the house and shivered a little from being wet, drying off the last of the water. My jeans were damp, but not soaked, thankfully.

Scarborough took care of the towels and brought me a pair of light sweatpants and a T-shirt. I went into the bathroom and changed clothes so Scarborough could dry what I had. He and I then settled on the sofa, and he nuzzled in close.

"You're cuddly all of a sudden."

Scarborough stiffened and I held him. "I guess I made up my mind, and…."

I turned, gently tilting his head upward. "I like it. You know that." He drew closer. "I like how you smell."

"Like horses…," Scarborough teased.

"Like a working man. I like that. There's no perfume or stuff like that about you. It's just who you are." I nuzzled the base of his neck, kissing him gently, and Scarborough quivered slightly next to me. Damn, he was so fucking responsive. That alone was a turn-on of epic proportions.

"I see. I never thought about how guys smell before."

I chuckled. "It's one of the strongest memory senses, and you smell good." I kissed him again, pushing him back against the sofa cushions as my passion rose by the second. God, he felt amazing, and I wanted nothing more than to strip him naked right there and lick him from top to bottom. But I doubted Scarborough was ready for me to do that in his living room, and I was too far gone at the moment to let him out of my arms.

"Martin," he whispered softly in my ear. "Do you think we can go to the bedroom? I put on fresh sheets and all that today."

I paused. "You were planning this?" I asked. Sometimes he surprised me no end.

Scarborough shrugged. "I may have hoped, but I wasn't sure. The stuff we did in Nebraska, well, you and I had been drinking, and I was scared if what happened was between us or if it was because of the drinking. And then you kept being nice and looking at me as though I was a buffet lunch, so I hoped that it was more than the beer. But I couldn't be sure, and then we got home and you acted like things were the same, but different. You watched me like I was different, but good different."

I swallowed hard. "What happened had nothing to do with the beer or anything else other than the fact that I wanted you. I still do. But the next morning you were distant and kept getting worse, and you kept saying that things would be normal when we got home. What the hell was I supposed to think?"

"I decided to invite you to dinner and see what happened," Scarborough admitted. "I figured I would know." A clap of thunder shook the house and then rumbled away into the distance. Beau whined and then settled in his place next to the sofa.

"Do you know?" I asked.

Scarborough hesitated, and then his lips drew upward into a sly smile. "I'm not really sure. But I thought trying a repeat of what we did in Nebraska might help me decide."

"Oh, you think so." I was already moving toward the hallway when another clap of thunder shook the house and the lights went out. I stood in near-complete darkness and drew Scarborough closer. I didn't need to see him to know where he was and how I felt about him. I cupped his face and brought his lips nearer to mine, taking them in a kiss, determined to make Scarborough understand that I wanted him and I would take him in whatever form he was willing to give.

The lights flashed back on, and both of us blinked. I stepped away and turned them out again. "Lead me to your room," I said softly.

Scarborough took me by the hand, and we got down the hall before another clap of thunder seemed to split open the sky. The lights stayed on this time, but it didn't matter.

We made it to the bed, and I lay back, tugging Scarborough down on top of me, while I feasted on his succulent lips. God, he felt good—solid, with heat radiating off him. I pulled at his shirt, desperate to get at his skin. He lifted himself up, and I got his shirt off, followed by my own. The storm outside slowly grew distant, the rain that pounded the room becoming gentler just as Scarborough seemed filled with electricity. Damn, he was hot, and seemed to grow more energetic by the second.

Scarborough ran his hands down my arms and tugged them away from his head and onto the bed. His eyes seared into mine with intense heat that grew exponentially. I waited to see what he would do, putting myself in his hands, and damn, he seemed to know exactly what I wanted. His lips took mine, and he stroked down my chest to pluck a nipple between his fingers, sending me damn near into orbit and making me groan with mind-numbing ecstasy.

"Am I doing something wrong?" Scarborough asked, his fingers stilling.

"God no." I pulled myself out of my sex haze and rose up to kiss him. "Believe me, I'll tell you if anything is wrong." The storm grew farther away as I kissed him.

After that, the weather didn't matter at all. A tornado could have carried us off to Oz, and I wouldn't even have known. Especially after the rest of our clothes had joined our shirts on the floor. Nothing separated Scarborough and myself except whatever barriers were put up inside, and I was determined to take as many whacks at those damned walls as possible.

Rolling us on the bed, I straddled Scarborough, looking down at him with flashes of lightning filling the windows as yet another storm cell drew closer. Not that I cared, since they let me see Scarborough's deep eyes better, even if it was only for a fraction of a second. "You...." My throat grew dry.

"How long have you thought… about us… together?"

I drew nearer, closing the distance between our lips, rocking my hips so I slid along Scarborough's length, and he hissed softly. Damn, I loved that sound. "I don't know. Mom put the idea in my head at her dinner… but she couldn't have… there had to have been something there, waiting for me to see what was in front of me." I kissed him as our hips came together, cocks sliding past each other in that ecstatic sexual dance that brought things into clear focus, at least for me.

Scarborough laughed at me. "Your mother…. At a time like this, you bring up your mother."

"You're the one who asked," I chuckled back at him.

"Yeah. But how am I supposed to—" He looked downward. "—keep things up when we're talking about her? Don't get me wrong, your mother is a lovely woman, but I don't want to think about her when I'm in my bed naked, with you… and…." Scarborough stammering and nervous was adorable.

"How about if I try something...?" I slid downward and engulfed him with my lips, sucking him deeply. Scarborough groaned, and I had to admit that all thoughts of my mother flew out the window and were carried away by the wind. It was that simple, and Scarborough moaned softly.

"Are you talking dirty to yourself?" I asked after backing away.

A gurgle bubbled up from Scarborough's throat as I stroked him. "Yeah...."

"You can say whatever you want." I loved dirty talk.

"Okay... then suck me!" He thrust his hips forward, and I took him deep. "Yeah... that's what I want. Take all of my cock." Just like that, I realized I'd created a monster, and fucking hell if it wasn't hot. "Jesus... fucking Christ. You're going to kill me."

I was good at this, if I did say so myself, and it seemed that Scarborough echoed those sentiments, rivaling the storm in his enthusiasm, which only sent my own desire into overdrive. I wanted to make him happy and drive him out of his mind. So many of the people in his life who should have cared for him had let him down, and I wasn't going to do that. I wanted to bring him joy. It was that simple, and from the way Scarborough's mouth hung open and his eyes glazed over, combined with how the dirty talk had given way to breathless moans and whimpers, I'd say I was doing a damned good job.

"Why are you smiling?" he asked when I pulled away. "Do you like torturing me?" He lay still, his countenance now a study in anticipation.

"Yes... and no. I want you to be happy, but I don't want this party to be over already." He panted, and I crawled upward until I could reach his lips. "I have to ask," I said, hovering just above his lips. "What do you want?" I stilled. "Close your eyes and tell me what you see in your mind's eye when you pleasure yourself. What is it that you imagine to make yourself go off?" He wasn't the only one who could do sexy talk.

Scarborough shivered, and I wondered if he was going to tell me. All these years alone, I figured Scarborough had to have used his right hand, but sometimes those things are intensely personal, so I was hoping that Scarborough would trust me with one of his fantasies so I could try to make it come true.

"I can't tell you that." He pulled away a little, and I figured I had my answer… on both counts. "What if you think I'm sick or something?" His cheeks reddened, and I grew more and more curious.

"We all have fantasies, things that our mind pulls up that we think are sexy. Some of them we want to try, and others are meant just as erotic fodder for our minds. You don't need to tell me one of those, but how about the first kind? Tell me something that you think about late at night that you want to try and see if it measures up." My arm shook with anticipation, and I settled on the bed next to him, letting my fingers wander over his strong chest. God, he was beautiful. Not in a conventional, model sort of way, but in a "man who has lived" way, with a few lines and marks on his skin that said that he'd lived a life of hard work and self-reliance. I just wished Scarborough knew how sexy that was… especially to me.

"Well…," he began and colored even more, though it was difficult to tell sometimes. And maybe the darkness that cloaked us now that the storms had passed was a good thing. "I always wondered…." He shifted on the bed. "I once saw this movie…."

"Did you like it?" I asked.

"Yeah…." He paused again. "What if my fantasies are boring?"

"And what if they're the same fantasy that I have?" I told him. "Like you, I knew how the birds and the bees worked because I was around livestock and saw horses and cattle fucking… not each other or anything." Hopefully a little humor would ease some of Scarborough's discomfort. "I knew the mechanics pretty quickly, and at one time, Mom had goats, but apparently the males she got were like us because they went after each other." I put my hand over my mouth. "I saw that boys could be together… at least in nature. I figured things out pretty fast."

"Me too," Scarborough said. "It's just that I don't think we can do what I thought about. I saw this movie where two guys did it in a sauna. They were both in there, they saw each other, and things progressed to them sucking and all kinds of stuff. The one guy cradled the other and practically bent him in half as he pressed into him. But what I remember was the way they looked at each other. It was so intense." Scarborough shivered, and I wondered if maybe he had given me the insight I was looking for.

"Give me a second," I said. I got up and went to the bathroom. Sure enough, in the corner was a small covered candle. Out here, candles were necessary if the power went out. Mom kept them in every room, and it seemed Scarborough used the same playbook. I found a match nearby and lit the candle, took it into the other room, and placed it on the dresser. It was surprising the amount of light a single flame gave off.

I rejoined Scarborough on the bed. "Now I can see you clearly." I worked my way between his legs and leaned over him. Huge declarations were most likely going to throw Scarborough off. Instead, I met his gaze with mine, looking into his eyes and slowly drawing nearer. "I've seen you for a while now." I kissed him and backed away. "I have to ask, in your fantasy were you the one on top or bottom?"

"Well…. The last time you were where you are now, and…."

I quivered with anticipation and excitement. "You want me?" I'd thought that would take a while. Scarborough giving up that kind of control was huge. I nodded. "Let me go see if I have the things we're going to need in my kit." I was pretty sure the stuff was out in the living room in the kit, which had been forgotten on the table just inside the door.

Sure enough, the battered travel kit sat where I had forgotten about it. I grabbed it and breathed a sigh of relief as I found what we needed.

When I returned to the bedroom, Scarborough lay on the bed, stroking himself, his legs spread in invitation, and I nearly dropped what I was carrying. "I figured I'd give you a show."

That was not what I had been expecting at all. Most of the time Scarborough was standoffish and kept to himself. Frankly, I had been expecting him to be more timid in bed, but damn, maybe I had unleashed some sort of monster… a wonderful, sexy monster. "Where did this come from? Not that I'm complaining." I crawled onto the bed, put the supplies on the bedside table, and pushed his hand away, replacing it with my lips, sucking him deeply as his musky headiness burst on my tongue. Man, Scarborough was like man candy, and I was already addicted.

"I…." Scarborough groaned deep and long. "You want me to talk when you're doing that?"

I chuckled around him and continued taking him, swirling my tongue around the head until he quivered under me. It was amazing.

"You're trying to kill me."

"No." I pulled back and reached for the sachet on the nightstand. "I want you happy and content." I slicked my fingers and teased the tender flesh of Scarborough's opening, lifting his legs and meeting his gaze. "Have you done this before?" I figured the answer and wasn't surprised when Scarborough shook his head. "Okay, do you want to roll over? It will be more comfortable for you. I know you won't be able to see me, but it should be a lot easier."

"No." He pulled me closer. "I need to be able to watch. I don't want to be disconnected."

"Okay." I grabbed a pillow and placed it under his hips to lift them and provide support to his lower back. Then I slid between his legs, leaned over him to meet his gaze, and captured his lips.

"I don't want to hurt you, so I'm going to take my time. If there's anything you don't like, just say so and I can stop." The last thing I wanted was for his first time not to be wonderful.

I teased his opening once more, using my fingers to excite him while I slid my lips over his cock once again. I wanted him to equate real pleasure with what I was doing, and when I slipped my finger inside him, he gasped, and I sucked him harder. Scarborough didn't seem to know where to focus, and that was pretty awesome.

"Martin," Scarborough breathed, as I continued opening him up.

By the time I was done, he was panting, and I was about to go out of my head with desire for this man. He was amazing, and the more I felt him and got to know him, the more he drew me to him. With Scarborough heaving for breath, I moved away, reaching for the nightstand. I rolled on the condom and then got into position, meeting his gaze.

"Are you really okay?"

"Yes. I'm ready." His eyes were almost glossy, and I pressed into him, taking his lips in a hard kiss. He gasped, and I held still, waiting until he was all right before sinking farther into his amazingly hot body. Scarborough pulled me in and moaned, arms sliding around my neck. "Is it always like this?"

"This is different for me," I said honestly, trying to keep my head from exploding with the heat and pressure around me. I could feel my heart and his heart. I wanted to stay like this with him, just the two of us forever. "It's so intense."

"For me too...." Scarborough whimpered, and I slowly began to move. "Jesus...." He groaned as I pulled out and then slowly pressed back in. "Do that again." He tightened his grip, and I kissed him, continuing to move with deliberate motions, trying to keep control of myself, because damn it all, I felt like a teenager. Being here with Scarborough felt so right, so perfect. Like I could give him what he wanted and needed, and he was doing the same in return.

"Oh, I will." I kissed away further conversation and moved more quickly, thinking unsexy thoughts for a few seconds to cool things just a little. Scarborough then pulled me back to him, and I nearly lost myself in his eyes. "Over and over again."

"More! I want more…," he gritted between his teeth.

"I know. But I'm not going to hurt you." I forced myself to go slowly, drawing out the pleasure as much as I could. I was experienced enough to understand that moments like this were something special, to be savored. "I won't. I want you to be over the moon."

"I think I already am…," Scarborough said, releasing me and grabbing my butt, his fingers digging into my cheeks, pressing me forward. Damn, I'd had no idea he was going to be this forward and demanding. It was sexy as all hell, and I moved faster, letting my desire and passion build higher and higher.

"I can't hold off much longer," I whispered, reaching for Scarborough's cock to stroke him as he arched his back, moaning softly in this symphony of passion that went from my ears and right down my spine. It didn't take long before I was flying, snapping my hips and gazing into Scarborough's huge eyes.

Everyone always said that the eyes were the window to the heart and soul, but I had never experienced that before now. It took my breath away. I could feel the beating of Scarborough's heart and his soul connected to mine, and I could feel his pleasure and knew the moment he let go and gave himself over to me. It was the most attractively sexy thing I had ever experienced in my life, and I knew I would fight for this man. If he tried to push me away once again, I wouldn't let him. He was worth it, and my heart wasn't going to take his walking away. That was frightening and amazing at the same time.

"I'm…."

I already knew he was close and tightened my grip, letting him tumble into his release as I plummeted into the abyss of blinding abandon.

Thunder began again, rolling in from the west and growing louder as I settled next to him and closed my eyes, drawing Scarborough into my embrace. I took care of the remnants of our lovemaking and lay still, letting the warmth and the glow of something wonderful settle around us.

"I didn't know things would feel this way," Scarborough whispered. "I mean… no, I don't know what I mean."

"Is it better than how you thought it would feel?" I asked, trying to help him.

"Yes. But I didn't have anything to compare it to until that night in Nebraska. I rarely did things to myself, and whenever I did, I felt dirty and a little stupid. I think Mom and Dad did a real number on me, and all these years it's been so easy to just deny that part of myself even existed. I lived here alone, and sex was something a person did to procreate, just like the animals. If I convinced myself of that, then I wouldn't feel so bad about being alone." Scarborough rolled over. "I was here, making a living and doing what I needed to do. I couldn't have children, so what good was sex for? It was pretty easy from there to just tell myself that I didn't need anyone else." He stroked my cheek. "But I was fucking wrong, and you changed that… and ruined all my well-laid traps and shit."

I nodded, knowing exactly what he was saying. If things didn't work out, Scarborough's emotional safety net had been pulled out from under him, the same as mine. There was nothing to catch us if we fell and our hearts shattered.

"I should put out the candle," I said softly, and got out of bed to blow out the light. I opened the bedroom door and then got into bed. I could almost feel Beau slinking into the room, and then he jumped up on the bed, settling near the bottom.

"Is Beau okay?" I whispered, and Scarborough hummed his approval.

It was so easy to let myself smile at this domesticity, the two of us in bed with the dog. It was like a weird heteronormative dream come true.

"Is it supposed to storm all night?" Scarborough asked, and I shrugged.

"I can check my phone, but I'm just going to be grateful for the rain and an end to this damned drought. We'll all need to assess any damage in the morning and figure things out. But for now, just relax and let's get some rest." Thankfully, this storm seemed to go around us, and the thunder never got close. I closed my eyes, but my head kept churning.

"You need to sleep too," Scarborough said.

I nodded. The room grew quiet and I tried to sleep, but I didn't want to miss a second of this. It wasn't so often that I was this happy. And I knew one thing from hard experience: when everything was going your way, it was time for the wheels to fall off the cart.

CHAPTER 9

"I SET up a time to go to St. Albans to talk about the problems I'm having with that club of theirs," Scarborough told me after I was done working with Storm on Saturday morning. "I hope Tuesday is okay."

"It's great." Storm was coming along, but he seemed to have hit a plateau. He still spooked and got anxious at the strangest times, and he shied from me about half the time and I had to approach him cautiously. And yet other times, he came right up to me. Still, I was hopeful that time and some proper care would continue to help him. But there was something I was missing with him. I was sure of it. Either that or Storm hadn't told me all that I needed to know. "I have about half an hour here with him, and then I'll put him in the barn. I brought some carrots for him as a treat." Storm loved them.

"You still want to go to the festival?" Scarborough asked. I had already collected and delivered the things we had decided to donate for prizes.

"Looking forward to it." I stopped Storm's exercises and let him rest, patting his neck gently. He was a great horse, and I kept coming back to the fact that he'd been mistreated and that I was still seeing the effects of it. "How about you?"

Scarborough nodded. "I'm a little worried," he said, leaning on the fence.

I finished the exercises and put Storm into a cooldown, letting him walk it off. Then I took him into the barn, where he had hay and water, gave him a few carrots, and praised him.

"Do you have things to do this afternoon? Or can you take an hour or two?" I closed the stall door, and Storm stuck his head out. I passed him another carrot and patted his neck. He seemed calmer in the stall than outside most of the time.

"What did you have in mind?" Scarborough asked.

"I thought you and I would go for a ride."

Scarborough snickered. "We did that this morning when we got up. Are you ready to go again already?" Damn, the gleam of mischief in his eye was adorable.

"I didn't mean that kind of ride, but we could do that too." I think now that Scarborough was letting go of some of his inhibitions, he was becoming a bit of a horndog. Not that I was complaining in the least. "I was thinking we could saddle up a couple of the horses and head out for a while. After all that rain, I want to check the levels in the creek and see how much bank erosion it caused." With rain that heavy, there was sure to be some. A few years ago, a storm of that magnitude put enough water in the creek that it threatened to cut a new channel, and unfortunately that could mean the creek could change course and leave our properties high and dry.

"Okay. I'll saddle a couple of horses." Scarborough hurried away, and I finished up with Storm. Now that he was nice and calm, I went inside the stall to see if he'd let me check his hooves. I didn't have high hopes, and sure enough, he was obstinate. At least he didn't try to kick me. I figured I was lucky on that count.

Beau began barking outside, and I left the stall once again now that Storm was settled. Beau stood just outside the barn as Clint got out of an old beater car. Beau stayed where he was. "What's up?" I asked him as the reverend climbed out of the driver's side of the car. Clint's father was at least six four, wide, imposing, and carried himself almost regally. "Good morning."

"Dad insisted he wanted to talk to you," Clint said softly.

"Has my son been causing trouble out here?" The reverend's voice boomed like he was giving a sermon on the rapture.

Scarborough joined me. "I believe the real problem is originating at the school where you're sending Clint," he said. "This Skull and Dagger Club."

I nodded my agreement.

"You're supposed to be studying and working hard. Not joining ridiculous clubs," the reverend spat. "You and I will be having a long talk about your behavior when we get home."

"Sir," I began, "Clint didn't actually do anything. He was supposed to get a hair from one of our horses as part of the initiation, but we stopped him. The horse they wanted him to approach is unpredictable, and Clint could have been hurt." I paused, waiting to see if my message was getting through. The reverend didn't turn to leave, so I thought I might have a shot. "It was other people who nearly caused the damage. Clint told us what was going on and has been helpful. You should be proud of him."

Those huge dark eyes glared at me. "And why is that?"

"Because... he stood up to them. That takes a lot and shows that you taught him right from wrong. Yeah, the two of you should talk, but I don't think it's the kind of one you think you need to have with him." I smiled, and the reverend's features actually softened.

"I don't fit in there, Dad. And I hate it. It's a military school, Dad, and you always preach that fighting isn't the answer." Clint turned away from the empty paddock. "I want to go to school in town, the same one that Jenny and Martha go to."

"It sounds to me like I need to have a talk with the people at your school," he said.

I figured I should go for broke. "Talking to your son is going to have a much better outcome, for both of you. Scarborough and I are meeting with someone at the school to put a stop to these escapades on his property."

The reverend nodded. "Clint, get in the car."

Clint sighed, and I waited until he was on the other side. "Sir, whenever my dad needed to have a serious talk with me, he and I usually had it on horseback. It was something both of us loved and it meant we were comfortable. Maybe head into town and stop at Twirly Whirly and get some ice cream or something." I could see the hardness creeping back into his features. "Clint is going to be old enough to make his own decisions soon. Maybe if you listened to what he wanted a little, those future decisions will be easier and he'll make the right ones." I stepped back, and he nodded and got into the car.

"Say hello to your mother for me," he said, started the engine, and slowly pulled out of the drive.

"Do you think he'll listen?" Scarborough asked.

I shrugged. "I hope so." I followed Scarborough inside and helped him finish the saddling, and then he and I were off across the fields toward the tree line that indicated the creek.

"When did you ride last?" I asked Scarborough.

"Other than to exercise one of the horses, quite a while ago, I guess. I don't have a lot of time to ride for pleasure." We didn't go fast, and Beau kept up with us as we crossed the open fields. The heat built and there was no relief from it until we passed under the trees. Instantly it was ten degrees cooler, and the deeper into the shade we went, the better it felt.

"You should try to find the time for fun." I figured that would need to be one of my missions.

"I just never seem to have enough time. There's always a huge list of things to do, and the animals need care every day. Your dad looking after things while I was gone was great, but I couldn't ask him to do all that needed to be done, so I'm still catching up."

The trail approached the creek, and we dismounted and walked the horses from there. The water was high and moving, but it wasn't dangerous. Still, I had hoped we might have a chance to swim, but with the water moving at that speed, it probably wasn't safe. I tied up the horse and got close to the water, sitting on a stump of a tree that had fallen some time ago.

"I used to go swimming just down there when I was a kid. Your place used to be the Gravelers', and they had a son a year younger than me. When it got hot, we used to come down here and go swimming. I haven't been in this area of the creek in quite some time."

"It must have been nice to have kids to play with."

I nodded as Scarborough joined me. "I forget that you didn't have much of a chance for friends outside school." It made me more than a little angry.

"When I was small, I thought it was normal. It wasn't until I got older that I realized that my dad thought of me as just some farm labor and little else." He sat still, and I put my arm around him. "You know, the thing is, I haven't thought of my dad a lot since I moved here, and now he crops up all the damned time. Maybe I can finally have things out with him when he comes and bring this whole issue to an end. I want to be able to tell him how I feel."

I turned to him. "How do you feel, deep down?"

Scarborough shrugged. "I don't talk about feelings. When I get upset, I work and keep busy. Always have. Bury the shit that bothers you and hope you forget about it and it withers and dies. That's how I've always done things." He turned and smiled. "I guess that hasn't worked very well. I had fifteen years to try to get rid of my dad's influence, with no luck."

"Do you hate him?" It seemed like a logical answer.

Scarborough paused and then sighed. "I don't think I know him well enough to hate him. I'd like to think that he isn't anything to me, but that isn't true either. I think of my father, and mostly I resent the things I missed." He leaned against me. "You met the people I went to school with, and they were pretty great. But I didn't have a chance to go on sleepovers or even camping trips the way the others did. I had work to do, and Dad kept me busy. I will admit that I never seemed to have time to get into trouble."

"But you didn't have much fun either," I supplied, and he nodded.

"What was it like for you? I know you had friends and got to do things."

"Yeah, I did. For a long time, Dad and I really didn't understand each other at all. I was a gay kid, out here in the country and scared half to death. I remember all the talk about Matthew Shepard, and I was afraid that if I told anyone, something like that would happen to me. Eventually I told my mom and dad, and it seemed to relieve some of the pressure between Dad and me. He must have figured that if I was gay, I was going to be different, and he let me. I have a lot of respect for him now." Things were pretty good between us, and I liked my dad. "He and I can be friends now."

"I'll never have that with my father," Scarborough said.

"It requires seeing each other as equals rather than just as father and son." I stood, pulled off my boots, and found a dry rock near the edge of the bank. I made room for Scarborough and dropped my feet into the cool, flowing water, sighing with relief. Scarborough joined me, and we dangled our feet, and when he turned my way, I kissed him.

The touch started out gentle but grew heated in seconds. Soon I had him in my arms, devouring his lips and wanting so much more. Damn, he just made me want to forget everything except him. "This is a little awkward, but…." I pressed him back, nuzzling at the base of his neck because there was just something about his scent that drove me out of my mind. Beau bumped my arm on the other side, and I straightened up, petting him as he nuzzled me, wanting his fair share of the attention. Not that Scarborough and I could do anything out here anyway. I figured the notion of sex outdoors, next to a stream, was pretty romantic, but the reality was that tender parts would be exposed to insects and the ground was wet enough that we'd get home looking like we'd fallen into a sty. Besides, as much as I wanted him, I'd much rather wait until it was just the two of us, in bed, and I could have all of him for as long as I damned well pleased.

We grew quiet, with the water and Beau filling the space around us.

"Sometimes I wonder if I'm good for anything other than work," Scarborough said, surprising me a little as he pulled his feet out of the water. "I'm prickly and don't understand other people very well."

"I don't think that's true. Think about how it was when you were at the reunion. You were a damned social butterfly. They loved you the entire time, and most everyone wanted to talk to you." I leaned against him. "It made me kind of jealous, if I'm being honest."

Scarborough scoffed. "I'm certainly no one to be getting jealous over." I sensed some nervousness in him, and Beau must have as well, because he shimmied over to Scarborough for some attention, resting his head on his leg. Scarborough lowered his feet into the water again while he stroked Beau's head. "I'm no catch, Martin. I never will be." He leaned back a little. "I certainly am not the kind of person who's worthy of someone's heart."

"Why?" It seemed like a strange thing to say.

"I wouldn't know how to treat someone I loved." Beau whined when Scarborough stopped petting, so he started again. "I think my dad loved my mom, but God, he treated her like she was a workhorse and pretty much ignored her and shit. They certainly aren't any kind of role models, and I never got to talk to them about anything important." He shifted to the side and then back upright again, like his butt was falling to sleep. Then he sighed and slowly stood, his feet and legs dripping onto the rock. I took that as a sign to stand myself and waited while my feet dried before pulling on my socks and boots. "We should get back." I could almost feel him withdrawing… getting further and further away by the second.

Once we had our boots on, Scarborough headed back to where the horses had been grazing. We mounted and started back. "What's going on in that head of yours?" I asked once we were both in the saddles.

"I'm not someone you should hang your heart on, Martin. I'm not. Trust me." He sat tense enough in the saddle that his horse shimmied under him.

"Why don't you let me decide what's best for me?" I wasn't having any of that noble sacrifice shit. That was about as dumb an idea as I had ever heard, and I could tell Scarborough was gearing up for something like that. "None of us knows what will happen tonight or tomorrow. So let's just take this thing as it comes and not get our undies in a wad."

Scarborough laughed. "Sometimes you have the best way with words. Have you ever thought of being a poet?" He was teasing.

"Sure. I'm working on a book. *Wadded Underwear and Other Poems*." I chuckled. "Maybe it would be a best seller and I could become a man of leisure." I got my horse to move faster and caught up with Scarborough, Beau bounding along nearby. He seemed content to explore and smell the smells, and I knew he'd stay pretty close.

"When we get back, I have some things to do." I half expected Scarborough to back out of the festival. "Do you want to pick me up or should I drive?"

"I have some things to do too. Why don't I pick you up about six? We can eat there and then see what fun we can have." I tried to be upbeat, but Scarborough seemed distant again.

"Okay." He came to a stop, and I brought my horse up next to his. "I don't know what I'm doing. I really don't."

"And you think I do? I've lived next to you for years, and there's no wild nightlife or a gaggle of gay guys running around town that you don't know about."

Scarborough's gaze seemed to stretch toward the horizon. "That's part of what I'm afraid of. There aren't many people around, so you're settling for me." He kicked his horse, and it surged forward, heading off to the barn at a gallop. I followed suit, and we raced across the field, not slowing until we approached the yard. Usually a headlong race would clear my head, but this one only left me more muddled than when we started out. Sometimes I wished I could make other people see things the way I did. Sometimes relationships were fucking frustrating.

I dismounted and led the horse into the barn, unsaddled him, and put him in the stall with water and food before wiping him down. "You know, Scarborough," I called, and got a grunt in response, "sometimes you're a real jackass."

"But what if I'm right?" he called as I closed the stall door and found him coming out of the stall across the way.

"What if you're wrong?" I countered, and leaned in to kiss him. "What if all this doubting and wondering is just you going in circles? What if I was meant to be in your life and you were meant to be in mine, and it took two pigheaded, stuck-in-the-mud cowboys fifteen years to figure out that the best thing possible in their lives just happened to be right next door?"

Closing the distance between us, I deepened the kiss for a few seconds, holding him tightly and figuring I'd do my best to fry his brain, because Scarborough sure had a way of making my own skip across itself. Damn, he tasted sweet, and I wanted to go caveman on him and drag him into the house to have my way with him, but instead I pulled away.

Flashing a smile, I turned and strode out of the barn. "Come on, Beau," I called, and finally turned back to where Scarborough stood, watching me. "I'll be here at six." God, I loved the befuddled expression on Scarborough's face as I climbed into the truck and took off. That should give him something to stew over for the rest of the day.

I SPENT much of the rest of the afternoon with a client who was trying to train a bad habit out of her horse, and it was not working. The horse was stubborn as hell and was not going to change his ways. Sometimes it was best if you knew when to throw in the towel, and I advised her to do just that.

"But I can't use him for competition with him acting that way," Lilly said, half in tears.

"I know. My suggestion would be to sell him and get yourself a horse that you can show the way you want to. He's a great riding horse, but he's too danged stubborn, and I have a feeling that I could work with him for years and he'll end up the same way." Just like people, once a horse picked up a bad habit, it was hard to unlearn it.

"But I thought you could do anything," she said with a huge sigh.

"People like to think so, but mostly I work with a horse to find a way to enhance what they do best. And Danny Boy here is going to be a great riding horse, but he'll only lead to disappointment in competition." I hated when I had to give people bad news.

"Okay." She seemed resigned.

"I think my dad has some horses that might work well for you. You could contact him. Danny Boy here is the kind of horse that most people want for trails and things like that, so maybe he can work with you." I knew she didn't have a huge amount of money, which was why she had gotten Danny Boy in the first place. He looked good, but he wasn't going to be right for her needs.

"I'll do that," she said, and I led Danny Boy into the barn and let her get him settled. "Are you going to the festival tonight?"

"Yes." I checked the time. "I need to pick up Scarborough. I got him to agree to come with me." I couldn't help smiling.

"I hear you have been spending a lot of time together." She shifted her weight from foot to foot. "Is he your boyfriend?" She latched the stall door and turned to me.

"I don't know what he and I are at the moment," I said honestly. "I think we're trying to figure things out."

She nodded, and I braced for the cold shoulder or something similar. I'd gotten it a few times, even though I had never tried to hide who I was. It still happened sometimes if the subject came up. "Good for you. I know you've been alone for a long time, and so has he." She left the barn, and I followed her. "Being alone sucks most of the time." She'd lost her husband to cancer a year earlier and was trying to keep things running without him.

"Yes, it does." I wished there was something I could do to help her. "Are you and Karen going?" Her daughter was eleven and a sweet girl.

"She wants to go," Lilly said without much enthusiasm.

"I'm picking up Scarborough at six, and we're going to eat there. If you want to join us, just text me and we can eat together if you like."

"I think Karen would like that. I was hoping this horse would be good for her to ride, but I'm going to have to get her another one." She seemed so defeated. "I'll talk to your dad and see if he can help me."

"Good. If Dad doesn't have something, he can certainly work with you to find a horse for her." Karen was a good rider, and as far as I had seen, she had the makings to be really great, but that required the right horse for her to partner with. "Message me and we can meet up at the festival." I said goodbye and headed out, checked in with another potential client, then went home to shower and change.

I managed to get to Scarborough's just before six, with Beau scolding me again with his big, sulk-filled eyes for leaving him at home. Scarborough was waiting for me outside and got right into the truck, and the two of us were off.

"You look good." I had rarely seen him in anything other than jeans, except at the reunion, and he had on a nice pair of tan pants with a light blue short-sleeve shirt.

"I wasn't sure what to wear, and I found this in my closet. Since we were going to town and stuff, I thought that maybe I should dress nicer." He pulled his seat belt on, one leg bouncing, which told me how nervous he was.

"It's really nice." I flashed him a smile and sped up, making the turn toward town, and found a parking space in one of the fields set up for cars. Lilly messaged that she and Karen were on their way, and I told Scarborough that they would probably join us at dinner. "It's the large tent right over there."

"Then let's go."

We joined the crowd waiting in line. This dinner was a tradition for so many people in town, and the scent of frying chicken hung in the air, enticing everyone. Scarborough's stomach rumbled, and I smiled.

"Hey, Karen," I said as Lilly's daughter found us first. She gave me a hug, and I introduced both her and Lilly to Scarborough.

"Mom said we were getting chicken. This is the best." She bounced on her heels. "Mom said you might go on some rides with me. She won't because she always gets sick." There were apparently a few rides just a block down the street.

"Sure." I met Scarborough's gaze, and he nodded and smiled as well. "I think we can survive some of the rides as long as this line starts to move before our stomachs think our throats have been cut." I winked at her and then turned to Scarborough, who was craning his neck to see around the rest of the line. He settled as the line began to move. It seemed whatever the bottleneck had been was fixed, because we started moving rather quickly.

"Why haven't I seen you around town very much?" Lilly asked Scarborough as we finally approached the front and picked up plates of golden-brown chicken, corn, and salad.

"I guess I keep to myself a lot," Scarborough answered softly.

It was simple, the chicken steaming hot, and for the hell of it, I got a second plate as an extra because I figured Scarborough was hungry. After we combined the food with a couple of beers and some sodas, the four of us sat down to a feast.

I knew the second Scarborough took his first bite. Damned if he didn't moan deep in his throat, and instantly my mind was back in his bedroom, the two of us alone, me buried inside him. I was fucking glad we were at a table because I would have embarrassed myself something terrible otherwise.

"People are staring," Scarborough whispered, and I looked up from my plate, meeting each stare with a glare of my own. Most people had the decency to turn away.

"I wonder what he does on that ranch of his all alone," someone behind me said. "I figure none of the cows or goats within a mile of the place are safe." A laugh followed, and I was seconds from teaching the fuckers some manners.

"You're just jealous," Lilly said as she whipped around. "Remember, Howard, you and I dated for a while." She wagged her pinkie, and the others at the surrounding tables laughed. "I suggest you keep your mouth shut. You got enough troubles of your own." She smiled brightly, and the laughter continued. "Damned asshole," Lilly said, then turned to Karen. "Forget you heard all of that and I'll buy you some ice cream."

Scarborough's mouth hung open, and he eventually returned to his dinner as the talk around us returned to normal and people went back to their own damned business. "I knew I should have stayed home," he whispered.

"Never let the assholes win," I muttered back. "No matter what. If the assholes win, then they think they're right. And from what I hear, Howard can barely tell his right from his left." I wasn't going to let Scarborough feel anything but supported. I put another chicken thigh on his plate and went back to my own dinner.

Scarborough held it together for a few seconds and then picked up his napkin, coughed, and burst out laughing. It was a wonderful, joyous sound that I wanted to hear over and over again as much as possible.

"Mr. Scar, are you and Mr. Martin boyfriends?" Karen asked, and the laughter stopped on a dime.

"You don't ask questions like that," Lilly said quietly.

I turned to Scarborough, who lowered his napkin and picked up a fork. He met my gaze, his eyes as serious as a bull rider at the rails. "Yes, we are."

I smiled, and Lilly sighed happily.

"My friend Jessica has two mommies," Karen said, and went back to eating.

I chuckled and glanced at Scarborough, who had returned to his dinner. Suddenly I wasn't so hungry. My belly did butterfly skitters, and I tried not to grin like an idiot. I mean, Scarborough had just told someone that I was his boyfriend. I had figured I was going to have to wait a long time before I heard those words, if ever. Reaching under the table, I squeezed his hand quickly, calming my belly, and then finished my dinner.

"When can we go on the rides?" Karen asked as soon as the four of us exited the tent.

"How about we play some of the games first?" I offered. Usually the games were local and run by the clubs. The groups had their booths like usual, but the carnival also had games. "Do you want Scarborough to win you something?" I whispered.

Karen nodded, turning to Scarborough with those adorable eyes. Of course, he couldn't say no, and soon enough Karen had a stuffed bunny as big as she was. Ultimately, Lilly ended up carrying the bunny, and we went on the rides. Afterward, she took Karen off to some of the club booths, thanking both of us for spending time with Karen.

"What would you like to do?" I checked my watch. "The fireworks will be in an hour, and there are still some games you haven't won." His ability to master the games of skill was incredible.

"Let's get a beer and sit down for a while," he offered, and I made my way to the food tent and got us a couple of drinks before weaving through the crowds of people to where he was sitting.

"You're some sort of freak, aren't you?" Howard was saying to Scarborough as I approached. "Look who's here. If it isn't fig and fag. Who the hell wants to have anything to do with either of you?" His words were slurred and he puffed his chest out.

I put the drinks on the table. "Go join your friends, Howard, and leave us alone. You've had too much to drink."

"Bullshit. What I want is to see you two butt-fuckers rode out of town. Especially the cow-fucker here." He reached for Scarborough, and I grabbed his arm, tossing it to the side.

"Go on home, Howard, before you do something you're going to regret." I tried to be calm, but my heart pounded in my ears, and I wasn't about to let anyone hurt Scarborough.

"I beat the shit out of you when we were in school, and I'll do it again, you little piece of shit." He pulled his arm back, and I snapped my fist to his nose. Blood spattered, and he abandoned his punch to grab his face to staunch the flow.

"I think that's enough out of you," I spat, and turned back to Scarborough. "Sorry."

Scarborough's mouth hung open. "I could have handled him," he said softly as Howard made his way out of the tent, holding his face in his hands. "You didn't need to do that." Scarborough picked up his beer and downed most of it.

I sat, sulking a little as I reached for my beer. "Yes, I did," I told him as he took a seat.

Scarborough shook his head. "Someone calls you a few names, and you go off like a Roman candle without thinking." He looked toward the tent entrance, and I followed his gaze. I half expected the sheriff to make an appearance, but instead it was my father who came over. He grabbed the chair across from us.

"I heard some commotion," he said, and I figured my dad had the right of it. I wiped my hand on a napkin and flexed my fingers. Dad looked between me and Scarborough. "You're the one who broke Howard's nose?" It occurred to me that he'd thought Scarborough might have done it.

"He deserved it," I said, and Dad nodded as Scarborough finished the rest of his beer.

"I don't doubt that." Dad fixed me with a look I couldn't quite parse. It might have been pride. "I'd say it's about time." Then he smiled slightly, knocked the table once, stood up, and headed for the line for beer.

I watched him go, trying to figure my father out. Though I was pretty sure that if he had been upset with me for what I'd done, he would have told me so.

I tensed when a hand landed on my shoulder and then disappeared again. I half expected someone to punch me as retaliation. A second patted my shoulder, and then a third as they passed. It seemed most people agreed that Howard had gotten what he deserved.

"You didn't need to fight him because he called you names," Scarborough said.

I set my glass down harder than I needed to and almost broke it. "Is that what you think?" I pushed it away and hefted myself up onto my feet. I needed to get out of this tent and into the fresh air. The festival had lost its allure for me, and maybe it was time to go home.

"What am I supposed to think?" Scarborough said as he strode up behind me, grabbing my arm. "Is this a new hotheaded side of you that I haven't seen before?"

"You've fucking known me for fifteen years," I told him as we headed out of the tent. It was definitely time to go home. "I don't go around punching people."

"Then why did you do it?" he demanded.

"Other than the fact that he was about to punch me? I wasn't going to let him talk about you like that. You deserve better." I whipped around and found myself face-to-face with an openmouthed Scarborough. "It's too bad I didn't rip his fucking head off, the asshole. He can say what he wants to about me—I don't care." I turned, striding through the dark street toward the field where I'd parked the truck. I weaved through the other cars, pulled open the door to my truck, and got inside, my temper still burning hot.

"You know, I can take care of myself," Scarborough said as he joined me.

"Yes. But I was pissed, and he was drunk as shit and wasn't going to stop. He had decided to shoot off his shit-assed mouth no matter what, and I put an end to it." I gripped the steering wheel in my hands, shaking it a little as some of the anger began to drain away. "Did you see the part where he was going to slug me, and the guy is way bigger than I am?" Reality was quickly setting in just how lucky I had been. Howard had always been a bully and bigger than everyone else. Might always made right in his book, and he had the size to back it up.

"You stood up for me?" Scarborough asked.

"Of course I did, you fool. You do that for people you care about," I retorted with a half smile. "He needed to shut the fuck up, though I probably would have been better off and my hand would ache less if he would have simply shut his mouth and gone on his way." I shook my aching hand, flexing my fingers, and then put the key in the ignition to start the engine.

"Stop…," Scarborough said, and I turned toward him before putting the truck in gear. He leaned over and kissed me hard, and my brain short-circuited in a matter of seconds. "No one has ever stood up for me before."

I cupped his cheeks in my hands. "Then it's about fucking time." I kissed him again, and then we pulled on our seat belts and I backed the truck out of the parking space and headed for home. As I reached the edge of town, the fireworks began, colored lights shining in the rearview mirror. Scarborough didn't turn around, and I continued driving and thinking as I tried to put yet another piece of the puzzle that was Scarborough into place.

"You know you don't have to fight people on my account," Scarborough said softly as we rode, the tires humming along the road.

"Maybe not. But you don't have to go it alone either. I'm here, and I'll fight along with you if you let me." I pulled to a stop at the sign and then passed through the quiet intersection.

Scarborough sighed. "I don't know how to let someone do that."

I stifled a sigh of my own, because that had to be one of the saddest things I had ever heard in my life. I wanted him to know that I'd be there in his corner, but then it occurred to me that after everything, maybe he was content to just go it alone. And that was frightening.

CHAPTER 10

ST. ALBAN'S school was maybe five miles outside of Red Rock. It had been founded as a small military prep school before my father had been born. The place had its own traditions and pretty much kept to itself. They were part of the greater community in a way, but as Scarborough pulled up to the gates with me in the passenger seat of his truck, I was struck by the fact that though I had driven by the place many times, I had never actually been on the grounds before. I wondered at the kind of reception we were going to get.

"I'm going to be happy to put this whole mess behind me, and after today, I hope I can go back to normal on the ranch and not have to worry about any more nighttime visitors." Scarborough actually hummed to himself, but something about the place made me nervous. Maybe it was the boys at the gate of the school acting like military guards rather than playing games the way most fourteen- or fifteen-year-olds did. Still, it wasn't up to me to tell people how their children should be raised.

"We have an appointment with Headmaster Talbert," Scarborough said, lowering his window.

"Yes, sir. Name, sir?" the young man asked in a very official way.

"Scarborough Croughton."

"Very good. Go right on through and around to your right and up to the main building. Commander Talbert's office is on the second floor at the top of the stairs." He stepped back, and Scarborough continued on, slowly following the directions.

The grounds were immaculately kept. A few boys walked the paths around the lawns, looking in a hurry to get somewhere. We found the imposing red stone building that looked like a cross between a castle and an armory, with a crenellated roofline. Like everything else, it was well maintained, and I wouldn't have been surprised if the entire place had been spit-polished.

"Jesus, this is something else," Scarborough said once we'd parked.

I craned my head to see all of the building once I was outside, and we headed up the steps and through the heavy doors. To say the staircase was imposing was an understatement, but up we went and found ourselves outside Commander Talbert's office.

"Look, I know you want to do this yourself, and I'll wait out here if you want me to." But something about the way the entire place was laid out seemed intended to project power.

Scarborough hesitated and looked around. He had to be as intimidated as I was. "I hate to ask…." He bit his lower lip.

"Then let's go. There's safety in numbers. I'll let you do the talking." I knocked on the door and stepped back, then followed Scarborough inside after being instructed to come in.

The office itself wasn't as big as I was expecting, but it was impressive. "What can I do for you, gentlemen?" he asked, standing to greet us. "I'm Commander Talbert."

"Scarborough Croughton, and this is my neighbor Martin Jamuson. He and I have uncovered an issue that I felt I needed to bring to your attention related to the Skull and Dagger Club. It seems that at least part of the initiation to the club requires that boys either approach one of my horses or that they need to get hairs from his tail." He paused, and I watched as the commander settled back in his chair.

"Gentlemen," he said gently, with a smile. "Sometimes boys will be boys, and their hijinks are hardly anything to worry about. The Skull and Dagger Club has been in existence at St. Albans for many years, and no one has ever been hurt. It's just a little high spirits in order to make sure the prospective club members are serious. It's nothing more than that." He placed his hands on the desk and plastered a smile on his lips.

Well, that got us nowhere. Talbert's dismissal caught in my craw, and I was about to step in, but he looked ready to say something more and I held my tongue.

"Say, maybe if you took a look around, you could see the campus and what we do here. It's our job to mold boys into men. That's our primary purpose here." He was clearly deflecting. A knock sounded, and the commander got up from his desk. "Please excuse me a minute. It's alumni week, and there are former students here on campus." He made his way around us.

I turned to Scarborough, understanding pretty clearly that we weren't going to get anywhere with this man.

The commander pulled open the door, and another man strode in. I got a look at him and did a double take, then turned to Scarborough, who had gone pale.

"Father," he said quietly. "What are you doing here?"

"It's alumni week, and I came over to visit and take part in some meetings here at the school," he explained. "When Commander Talbert told me you had requested a meeting, I asked to be included."

Scarborough tensed. "You went here?" he asked. "I knew you went to a military school, but I don't remember you mentioning St. Albans." He was clearly taken aback, and I wondered just what was going on.

"The school has a history going back nearly a hundred years, but it underwent a name change about twenty years ago. It used to be Milford Military Academy." The commander took his place behind his desk once more, and Scarborough seemed completely overwhelmed and stared at his father.

"I'm sorry, but his being here isn't germane to why we're here. You have students who are putting other students in danger and at risk with the initiation to the Skull and Dagger Club. I would think you'd be more concerned about their welfare," I explained. Scarborough didn't seem to know where to look.

Scarborough's father walked around and stood next to the commander's desk. "The Skull and Dagger Club is part of how St. Alban's molds boys into men. I know it did for me." He turned and met the commander's gaze, then turned back to Scarborough with a smile.

"Neither of you needs to worry. I'll look into this matter personally and make sure that no students are tasked with anything remotely dangerous, and you are not going to have to worry about your horses and anyone on your property." Now he was simply trying to get rid of us. "I can assure you of that." He stood, and I got the impression we were being dismissed.

Scarborough mumbled a goodbye and left the office. I followed, then turned back at the door. "You need to do more to keep your students safe. They are putting each other in danger for the sake of some stupid club." I glared at the commander. "If you don't, I'll turn you in to the state education board, and they can see if your license should be pulled." I patted the doorframe and left, catching up to Scarborough, who was already at the doorway outside. "You didn't know your dad went here?"

"No. But that explains the visits to Red Rock as a kid. He was coming back to be part of the school or for alumni events, and he didn't want Mom and me with him." He reached the truck, got in, and drove off the grounds as quickly as he could before flying down the country roads. "I can't fucking believe him. I was in the same room as my father, and all he could do was take the side of the damned commander and some stupid club that he was a member of when he was sixteen." Scarborough gripped the wheel tight enough that his knuckles turned white. "I wish to hell I had just told him off." He slowed down and eventually pulled off to the side and came to a stop, banging the steering wheel with his palm.

"What is it?"

"Fucking hell. I should have let you handle this. I sat in the same damned room with my father and was too intimidated to say all the things I wanted to. I haven't seen him in fifteen years, and there was so much I could have said. But...." He gripped the wheel and ground his teeth.

"Let it out," I told him. "Yell if you want."

Scarborough's phone rang, and he answered it. The voice was loud enough that I could hear it.

"What the hell were you trying to do today? Embarrass the shit out of me? It's bad enough you don't give a shit about the family farm, but you had to be a big wimp and run crying because a few kids might have been on your pathetic little farm. What the hell is wrong with you?"

Scarborough sat still, stunned once again.

I wanted to reach through that damned phone and wring the man's neck. I nearly took the phone from Scarborough, but held my hands to myself. It was my instinct to try to help the people I cared about, and seeing Scarborough this upset and feeling exactly what he was in my gut told me how deep my feelings had grown. I would fight for him over and over again, and God damn anyone who tried to hurt him.

"I'm so relieved I never sent you to St. Alban's—"

Scarborough's hand shook as he pressed the red button on the phone to end the call.

The cab of the truck grew quiet, and I opened my door, got out, and walked around to Scarborough's side of the truck. "Let me drive," I said gently, and he climbed down.

Once we were buckled in, I pulled back onto the road. Scarborough sat without saying a word the entire way back to his ranch. Frankly, I was worried. When he was angry, the hurt and frustration came out. With him sitting silently, I knew he was holding the damned hurt and frustration inside, probably trying to cowboy up and bury it. I understood that, I really did, but it wasn't healthy. And it meant that at some point, Scarborough was going to blow.

When I pulled in, he got out of the truck and stomped to the porch without looking back at me. I determined I wasn't going to be hurt, and instead I went to Scarborough's barn just to check that everything was okay in order to give him some time to himself. When I left the barn, I expected Scarborough to come back out, but the front of the house remained quiet. I texted him to find out what was going on.

I can't talk now. I'll call you later, he replied.

Disappointed, I got into my truck and drove home, hoping he would be okay and wondering what the hell was going through his mind. I figured that Scarborough was hurt because of his father, but I was also afraid that he was pulling away and back into his shell. The hardest thing was that if he was, there was little I could do about it. Hurt but trying not to let it eat at me, I headed for home to give him some time.

CHAPTER 11

"MOM, I don't know what to do," I said, sitting on the navy blue slipcovered sofa in her living room. She leaned back in the light blue wingback chair that had been her place to sit for as long as I could remember. "It's been two days, and when I call, it goes right to voicemail, and if I send a message, I get a response, eventually, saying that he's really busy working." I leaned forward. "I know he's turning into a turtle because of that father of his. What the hell do I do?" It was driving me crazy.

Mom nodded, completely unruffled by my outburst. "Of course, honey. You love the man, and it hurts that he's shutting you out. But remember this: the issues with his father that you told me about go back a lot further and are a lot deeper than you think. And you can't do this for him. He needs to figure it out for himself."

Hell, I hated when she was right, and I clutched the arm of the sofa, the fabric smooth under my palm. "But what do I do?"

She sipped her tea and nodded as though she knew something I didn't, which was more frustrating. "Give him another day. That man is crazy about you too."

I shrugged, because that didn't add up for me.

"Anyone with eyes can see it. He looks at you like you're spun sugar." She grinned. "Tomorrow, you go over and see him. He needs a chance to think things over, but he also needs to know that you aren't going to be scared away or bolt at the first hint of something hard. Okay?"

I sighed. At least it was a plan, and that gave me something to think about. Now I just had to figure out what the hell I wanted to say to him.

I GOT some unexpected help the following day when I went to Scarborough's on my way back from town, planning to work with Storm or at least use that as an excuse to be there. His truck was out front, and the house doors were closed. The barn door was open, so I went in to see if he was there. The door to Storm's stall wasn't closed. I checked the paddocks and then raced to the house.

I knocked and pushed the door. It was open. "Scarborough, Storm is out. His stall door mustn't have been latched fully, and he's loose," I called just inside the door, and saw him jump up from where he'd been sitting in one of his chairs, just staring. I hurried back to the yard to check for any sign of the horse while calling my father. "Dad, Storm's gotten out. We need your help." Whether Scarborough wanted me to or not, I was going to try to do what I could.

"Your mother and I are on the way."

God, I loved both of them for that. I was fucking lucky. Mom and Dad were solid. They didn't always agree with me, but they had my back. I wished Scarborough had that same family background.

"Any sign of him?" Scarborough asked, coming outside as he too looked around.

"No. Mom and Dad are on their way. I didn't see him near the road coming from town. Why don't you go back that way just to check? I'm going to saddle up one of the other horses and head out toward the creek. I'll have Mom stay here and man the ranch in case he comes back. Dad can head out past my place and his place." I sure as hell hoped that horse wasn't panicked and injured somewhere. "Call if you see him, and we'll do the same."

"Okay. Thanks." Scarborough got in the truck and took off, turning out of the drive as Mom and Dad approached the ranch. I gave them their instructions, and Mom came with me to help with the other horses while I got my ride saddled.

On the same horse I'd ridden before, I headed out across the fields toward the creek. I was hoping that Storm might have gone toward the water, though it was far more likely that as soon as he was free, he would take off in whatever direction he happened to choose. I kicked my horse forward toward the rise, hoping I could get a better view of the area. I pulled my horse to a stop at the top and looked over the surrounding fields. The land seemed so peaceful, and a ride like this would be so wonderful if I weren't out looking for a lost horse. I tried to think where Storm might have gone if he were actually thinking rationally rather than just running headlong. I headed down off the rise and back toward the creek.

My phone buzzed. "Anything?"

"No," Scarborough reported. "Are you finding anything?"

I continued riding and paused. "Maybe," I said, seeing tracks in a few places where the soil was still soft from the rain. I looked back toward the house and then out to the tree line. These tracks were too far away to have been made by Scarborough and me the other day. "I'll holler if I see anything more," I promised, and ended the call, heading in the direction of the tracks. It wasn't much to go on, and the tracks disappeared, but I continued looking for any sort of sign or something to follow as I went off to the north and west.

Messages came in from Dad and another from Scarborough that they hadn't seen anything. I responded that I might have seen tracks, but that was all. The creek turned at the edge of Scarborough's property, and I headed over that way. The trees were extra thick there, and the land rather shallow and sometimes prone to flooding during heavy rains. As I came around the curve on the open land, there stood Storm at the tree line, munching on grass as though he hadn't a care in the world.

I sent a message to everyone else that I had found him and then called Scarborough with the good news. He was relieved to say the least. After hanging up, I tied my horse to a tree, took the long lead I'd brought, and approached Storm slowly, speaking softly so he had to strain to hear my tone. I wanted him curious enough about me, and sure enough, he allowed me to approach him.

Storm was nervous, but I soothed him as best I could, talking to him and patting his neck while I led him over to the other horse. Thankfully, he seemed content to follow, and I was able to tie his lead to my saddle, remount, and walk back toward the ranch.

I have him, I texted to Scarborough, but didn't get a response, which I thought strange. I sent another message and put the phone in my pocket, turning back to Storm, who appeared to want to get home. I was well aware that if he decided to bolt, there was little I could do to stop him. But at least we were moving in the right direction.

The silence to my messages worried me. Scarborough would be on edge until I got his horse back, and knowing him, he'd have his phone in hand waiting for the next message.

When my phone vibrated in my pocket, I pulled it out, expecting Scarborough, but it was my mom. "What's up? I have him."

"Trouble. Scarborough's father just showed up apparently. Scarborough is on his way back, I think. I tried calling, but he isn't answering, probably driving."

"Yeah. I'm on my way back." I looked up toward the ranch house. "You can probably see me coming across the back." I sped my horse up a little bit, and Storm came along easily. I hoped I got there before Scarborough did.

When I finally reached the yard, it was quiet. Scarborough slowly pulled into the drive, and I got Storm into his stall and made sure it was well locked.

"Thank you," Scarborough said as he came in the barn.

"It's okay. I'm glad I found him."

"There's a strange car in the yard, and…." He turned back toward the door.

I closed the second stall door and hurried to him. "Mom called. She tried calling you, but you didn't answer." I swallowed hard. "Your father is here."

"Shit," Scarborough said softly. "I don't want to talk to him. I've done enough of that in the past few weeks, and there's nothing more that we need to say to each other."

I took his hand. "Then don't. I'll tell him to be on his way. If he doesn't leave, the sheriff can see that he does."

Scarborough shook his head. "I…." He sighed deeply.

"Sit down," I said softly, and we took seats on a couple of bales of hay. "You don't have to see him again… ever. Not if you don't want to. But I think you have some things you want to tell him. Maybe need to say to him." I took his hand, threading his fingers with mine. God, I loved the simplest touch of his skin.

"I can talk to him on the phone, but every time I see him in person, I feel like I'm fucking sixteen years old again. And I hate it. I've taken care of myself for years. I have my own ranch and a life that has nothing to do with him. I never asked him for anything, and I've worked hard my entire life." He turned to me. "What the hell did I do wrong for him to treat me the way he does?"

I wished I had an answer for him. This was his decision, and he had to decide what actions he was going to take. "You can do whatever you want to do. But I want you to know something." I touched the side of his head. "Not up here." I moved my hand to his chest. "But here."

He shrugged. "I don't get it."

"Follow your heart, babe. If you want to have it out with him, then do it. If you want to punch the bastard in the teeth, then make sure you're listening to what your heart needs, not just your head." I squeezed his fingers. "Look, I will be here no matter what you decide, and in the end, you can refuse to see him, let him go, and I'll still love you just the way I do now."

Scarborough did a double take.

"Yes. You heard what I said, and I meant it. You don't have to say it back or anything like that." Though it would be damned amazing to hear those words. Honestly, I wasn't sure how Scarborough felt about me. We spent a lot of time together, had fun, and spent most nights in the same bed, with Beau sleeping at our feet. It was so easy to imagine that he thought of me as special. "But I wanted you to know that you aren't alone. That you have people who care for you and hold you, Scarborough Croughton, in their heart." God, I was sounding like a character in the romance novels my mother read. Hell, maybe I'd picked it up through osmosis.

Scarborough pulled away from me and held his head. "I don't know if I can do this. I know you think I should see my dad, but…."

"Then don't." I meant what I said, even though I knew that it was eating him inside. After the way Scarborough had reacted in the truck after leaving the school, I knew in my heart that he needed to confront his father and clear his chest and his soul. Even if it consisted of a punch to the guy's gut. "Like I said, I will still be here, and so will Mom and Dad. You'll come to dinner, and you and I will still go riding and to festivals and do all the things we've done." I leaned closer. "And I'll sleep in your bed and you'll sleep in mine. Nothing will change as far as I'm concerned." I stood up and moved away. "Whatever you decide, do it for you and your own peace of mind." I walked toward the barn door. "Mom is inside with your father. I'm going to perform a rescue."

"Dad isn't going to hurt your mom," Scarborough said.

I scoffed. "If your dad acts the way he did at the school, I'm afraid for him. Mom can take care of herself." I left the barn, went up on the porch, and went inside. I found Mom sitting in one of the living room chairs with a glass of tea that she must have brought with her, Scarborough's father sitting across from her, as rigid as a board.

"I told your dad that we found the horse, and he went on to a client he wanted to meet." She glared at Mr. Croughton.

"Where is Scarborough?" he asked impatiently.

"This is his home, and I'm sure he'll be in when he's ready," Mom said. "Your manners certainly need a brushup." She never raised her voice, but the steel in her tone was hard to miss.

"You know what he is…?" Mr. Croughton continued, and Mom leaned forward as Scarborough opened the door.

"I'm well aware of who Scarborough is. It seems to me that you're the one who knows nothing about your son." She stood and put her glass on the table beside the chair, then headed for the door. She smiled and patted Scarborough on the cheek as she passed. "I'll be out in the barn. I need some time with the good part of the horse." The implication was clear that she'd already spent time with a horse's ass.

I shook my head and took the chair Mom had vacated. "You must have been quite something to make my mom that angry with you." I leaned forward. "That's impressive." *In a severe asshole sort of way.*

Mr. Croughton shifted his weight and looked up at Scarborough. "You and I need to talk."

Scarborough half looked like he was about to leave the room, but his shoulders squared and his expression hardened. "Yeah, I think we do." He glanced at me and then sat in the other chair. "Martin is going to stay."

"You not man enough to talk to me on your own? This is a family matter." Damn, Mr. Croughton was one self-entitled prick.

Scarborough looked as though he was about to lose his cool. "Martin is family." And just like that, I knew how Scarborough felt. "What is it you want to say? I'll give you two minutes. Then I get my say, and you better be prepared to listen." Scarborough got to his feet. "I left home right after high school because you couldn't take the fact that I was gay. I made my own way for years and worked myself to the bone, just like I did at home." Apparently Mr. Croughton's two minutes had evaporated. "I saved and bought myself a place here." He stalked closer to his father. "You never gave a damn about me. All you wanted was someone to work on your farm, and when I was gone, you had to do it."

"The farm is safe now, and—"

"I don't care about it. That farm only reminds me of you. And I don't care about your opinion or what you think. You're nothing. I have a family here, people who care about me, and they're worth more than you will ever be." He took a deep breath. "I'm not sixteen years old anymore, and you don't get to tell me what to do or boss me around. I'm my own man, and you have no say in it." He stood straighter and taller than he had in a while, and it was fucking sexy.

Scarborough drew closer to his father, and I could no longer see his expression, but the tension in his body was tight as a guitar string. "I realize now that while you are my father, you never really loved me. That was something you were never capable of doing. After I left, I spent a lot of years alone because I didn't think I was good enough." He turned to me and his gaze softened. "I've been here for fifteen years, and it took me all that time to realize that I'm not alone. I never was once I moved here. I had friends." He turned back to his father. "Whatever you want or think you need from me…." He shook his head. "I'm not your son any longer, and I don't need you for anything. I haven't in a very long time. I have a family of my own… here… and you can go back to Nebraska and back to the same house and rot there for all

I care." Scarborough stepped back. "Now I think it's time for you to leave, and I don't want to see you again… ever. I'm through with you. It's been almost twenty years since I had to leave, and I don't want or need you in my life." Scarborough's shoulders slumped a little, and he sat back down. He looked wrung out and tired.

"I think that's your cue to leave," I said.

"I have something to say."

I had lost patience with this self-centered bastard. "This is his house and you have no power or rights here. I suggest you go because he asked you to. The sheriff won't be as nice. Have a safe trip back to Nebraska." I went to the door and opened it, then closed it behind Mr. Croughton, watching to make sure his car turned around and left the yard.

I sat back down, and Scarborough sat back in the chair, closing his eyes. "I feel better. Fifteen years of shit held inside."

"Are you okay?" Mom asked as she came inside, going right over to Scarborough.

"Yes. I'm better than I have been in a while." He actually smiled and held out his hand. I took it, and my mom grinned like the cat who ate the canary. "I think Martin and I have some talking to do, but not right at this moment. But soon." He was still smiling, and I must have been grinning like an idiot, because Mom sat down with a satisfied expression on her face.

"I'm glad, honey." She patted Scarborough's shoulder. "I'm happy for both of you." She walked around me and picked up the glass she'd left earlier. "You boys come to dinner tomorrow night. I want to make a nice meal. Both of you need some meat on your bones. I swear you don't eat enough."

"Do you want me to take you home?" I asked.

"No. Your father is on his way back, and he'll stop by. You two enjoy some quiet time together, and I'll see you tomorrow." She went outside, leaving us alone.

"I can't believe your mom is okay with this... us." He was almost shaking.

I laughed outright. "She was trying to get us together the last time she had you over for dinner. I think Mom saw something in each of us that neither of us did." Dang, I never thought I'd be happy my mother was a meddler.

I squeezed his hand and sat back, just wallowing in the happy for a while. A vehicle pulled into the drive, and I checked out the window as Dad came to a stop. I expected him to get Mom and go home, but they knocked and came inside.

"Is something wrong?" we both asked, sitting up.

Dad nodded and came inside, with Mom behind him. "I made a few discreet inquiries with the auction company you bought Storm from, and I found out a few things. His name was Charcoal Briquette."

We both made a face.

"Yeah. That was awful. I was able to look a few things up, and I found out that he was owned by a family a hundred miles west of here. Because of confidentiality and the fact that my friend broke the rules in telling me this information, I didn't contact them, and I won't give you their information either. I did put a call in to a friend. The farm that Storm was on was horrid. The animals were seized by the county for cruelty and payment of taxes. Apparently they had a reputation for not having enough money to care for the animals, so they simply made them wait until they could afford to feed them." Dad looked green around the gills. I thought I was going to throw up.

"So no experiments or anything?"

"No. Just poor treatment and abuse, as far as I can tell. The son was charged with animal cruelty and found guilty. He was jailed because it was a second offense." Dad seemed a little unsteady, and I gave him my chair. Dad didn't get emotional about a lot of things, but horses were as big a part of his heart as Mom or me.

"But why did I get him for a song?" Scarborough asked.

"Because it was rumored that he was abused. You just didn't hear it, I believe. And look at the horse you got because of it." Dad took a deep breath. "It will take some time, but his memories will fade, and as long as you and Martin treat him right, he'll get better and better."

"No one was trying to steal him or anything like that?" I asked, and Dad shook his head. "Sometimes our imaginations can get the better of us." I half snorted. "I'm relieved, though. I can work with him, and we can regain his trust. He's young enough that he will be a good horse someday."

Dad chuckled. "Check out his bloodline when you get a chance. I'll pay plenty of money for one of his colts someday. They could be champions." He grinned like he'd won the lottery. "When the time comes, I can help you book clients. I also suggest that you breed him with some of the stock that we already have. That way we can see the kind of colts he breeds. I bet we could get a good price for each of them."

"Dad," I warned.

"This is my business, and I know what sells. And provided he passes on his good characteristics, he could be a real moneymaker." Dad was as excited as I had ever seen him.

"So how do we prove his bloodline?" I asked. "His name was changed."

"True. But now I know where to look. You leave that to me. I'm good at this sort of thing. I can prove who Storm is. You and Scarborough continue working with him so he shows well and calms down, and then we'll see about getting this party started." He sat back. "I'm also willing to bet that once he starts getting his rocks off on a regular basis, he'll calm down some as well."

I looked at Mom, who rolled her eyes.

"Would either of you like some iced tea?" Scarborough offered.

"No thank you, dear," Mom said. "We need to be going. You two have had a busy day, and there are still chores that have to be done at home." Mom stood, and Dad followed, both of them saying goodbye and Scarborough seeing them out.

"I'm glad no one used him for experiments or anything," Scarborough said when he returned.

"Me too. Though it sounds like he had a hard enough life. But with good treatment and some care, he'll be okay." I stood and took Scarborough's hand. "Sounds like someone else I know."

Scarborough nodded. "I guess I didn't realize how much I needed to have someone in my life until I had someone in my life." He sighed and pulled me into a hug.

"No more pulling away?" I asked as he held me tightly. "You know, being close to someone does have its advantages." I slid my hands down his back to cup Scarborough's tight cowboy butt.

Scarborough nodded. "I still have work to do, Marty," he said, but didn't back away. I loved the way he said my name because I knew what it meant inside his head. If he cared enough for a nickname, then…. I swallowed and pushed away the rest of the mushiness.

"I know. I do too. And as much as I would like to stay right here and feel you up, the chores aren't going to do themselves. So how about you come over for dinner? I'll cook us something and we can talk." I closed the distance between us to take his lips in a gentle kiss that grew heated.

Damn, it startled me sometimes how things between the two of us could go from zero to sixty in a few seconds. I hoped that lasted forever, though working with a hard-on was bad enough. I was grateful that at least I didn't have to ride with one.

Thankfully Scarborough pulled back, because my willpower was draining fast. "I'll be there about six thirty?"

"Good deal." I had to go now or I wasn't gonna make it out the door. With a sigh, I took one last look at Scarborough with his just-kissed lips and half-lidded eyes. He turned to me, gaze heating right up again. I hurried back to him, put him in a clinch, and kissed the hell out of him. He whimpered, and that was almost my undoing. I was so damned hard, and every fiber in my being said to just stay and take him right there on the living room floor. I backed Scarborough up past the coffee table and lowered him to the sofa.

"You better go," Scarborough breathed without releasing me.

"Oh, screw it. The chores will wait. I want you more than—"

Scarborough patted my shoulder. "Your animals need you to make sure they're okay. I'm not going anywhere, I promise you that. God, I don't think I'm going to be doing anything or going very far without you for a very long time."

Those words were like music to my ears. I forced myself to back away, blinking, my head spinning. Years—it seemed like I had waited years for someone to say something like that to me. I had pretty much given up hope, and fuck, the answer and what I had been looking for was right next door all the time.

"Okay." I got up and took a step back, breathing deeply to clear my passion-addled head. "I'll see you tonight."

I swear I don't remember the ground under my feet as I went to my truck, or very much about the drive home. I do know that Beau was happy to see me, and he and I did our chores together and I fed him. But other than that, the rest of the day was a blur, with my thoughts centered almost solely on Scarborough.

AT SIX thirty on the nose, a knock pulled me out of the kitchen and away from the pork chops I was making for dinner. I opened the door to Scarborough in full cowboy hotness—jeans, red shirt, hat, buckle—and carrying a bouquet of wildflowers. "I thought these could be nice for the table." He seemed shy as he thrust the flowers into my hand. "Too girly?" he asked.

I couldn't help smiling. I had never in my life thought that anyone would ever bring me flowers. "They'll look very nice."

He handed me a six-pack as well, as I stepped back to let him come inside.

Beau greeted him with wagging butt and excitement while I put the flowers in a jar, because it was all I had, and finished up dinner.

My hands shook, I was so damned nervous and excited. Nervous because I didn't want to screw this up, and excited because there was something there to potentially screw up. Not that I was in the habit of messing things up. When it came to relationships, there wasn't a great deal of experience there. And I was jittery because this was new and….

"What are you doing in here, mumbling under your breath?" Scarborough asked, his hands sliding around my waist. Beau settled nearby, and I leaned back into Scarborough's embrace. "You're shaking."

"Sorry." I did my best to tamp down my nerves.

"Nothing to be sorry for." He held a little tighter. "I guess I'm not the only one who's gotten all wound up lately."

"Nope." I closed my eyes and let the warmth sink into me. "I'm just hoping that things can settle down again."

"Me too." Scarborough nuzzled the base of my neck, and I stretched to give him better access. After a kiss, he pulled back and his hands slipped away. "Is there anything I can do to help?"

"Dinner is almost ready. I need to put the chops on, and then I can get the rest out." The food wasn't complicated—pork chops, a salad, and some fresh beans I'd gotten at one of the farm stands. That was one of the lovely things about living out here. When the gardens came in, we had plenty of fresh things to eat. I got the chops cooking and the beans in a pan with a little water, and I was pretty good to go. I set the salad on the table as Scarborough got plates and silverware.

We worked companionably, with Beau underfoot almost the entire time. "Go on and lie down. I know you're looking for scraps, but there aren't going to be any and you'll get fed in a little while."

He wasn't a beggar, but Beau was ever hopeful that a juicy tidbit would hit the floor.

"Man, that was good," Scarborough said as he sat back in his chair, lightly patting his flat belly.

I took care of the dishes and got them into the dishwasher. Then I fed Beau, and Scarborough and I went into the living room.

"Should we talk first?"

"You know, sometimes talk is overrated," I teased.

"Maybe." He plopped down on the sofa, and I sat next to him, slipping off my shoes and resting my socked feet on the table. God, that was comfortable. "But I think it's something we need to do." He rested his hand on my thigh, and my entire attention centered there. "I guess we should talk about where we see this going."

"Okay." I turned toward him. "What do you want, honey?" Sometimes things were just that simple.

"I never pictured my life with anyone else. That was something I thought was closed to me. So I don't have any huge dreams or expectations. I guess I thought we might live together, but we each have a house, so I'm not sure where. I don't want to give up my ranch, and…."

"Me either. We could spend time in both and see which one feels right. I don't care which one we live in, if I'm honest, as long as I get to go to bed next to you and see your face in the morning." Everything else was easy as far as I was concerned. "Maybe we could look at expanding the ranch. The land on the other side of you is going to be for sale soon. Pool our resources, add some land, run more cattle, grow what we have. Maybe eventually live in your place, and if we hire someone, they could live in the house here." There were lots of options as far as I was concerned. "I guess I thought we would talk about us."

Scarborough nodded. "I'm just a cowboy. Nothing more."

I held him tighter. "You're wrong about that. You're much more than just a cowboy, because you're my cowboy, and I intend to keep you forever." I held his gaze until he nodded slightly, his lips drawing upward.

"I want a family and a home, maybe a chance at a good life, and maybe someday to retire and go someplace warm when the winter makes my bones ache." He leaned closer. "I want nights like this where you and I sit in the winter, the wind blowing, and yet inside it's warm and…." He turned to me, and I gently touched under his chin. He smiled and drew nearer, closing the distance between us. "I think the most important thing that needs to be said is that I've come to love you, Marty. And I want you forever too." We sighed together. "I don't say what I'm feeling very often. Heck, I've probably talked to you more in the last few weeks than I have to most anyone else in my life."

"Why is that?" I asked.

"Maybe because I have something I want to say to you. I think it's also because I love it when you talk and I gotta talk to get you to." Now that was circular logic.

"Just promise me we'll talk about the things that are important to us. No stalking off and expecting the other to know what we're thinking." I leveled my gaze for a second. "I love you too."

Beau jumped into the nearest chair and curled into a ball, resting his head on his tail and blinking at us. I turned away from him and got lost in Scarborough's eyes. Closing the distance between us, I kissed him, and he wrapped his arms around me. Heat instantly blossomed between us, and I gasped for breath, holding on to Scarborough for all I was worth.

"Let's go into the other room," he whispered.

I stood, taking him by the hand, leading him down the hallway to my bedroom. Beau jumped to the floor and I knew he was following, but I closed the door before he could come inside.

Scarborough sat down on the edge of the bed to take off his boots and socks. I pounced on him as soon as he was done, tugging at his shirt as he drew me closer. This was the thing in my life that I hadn't known I was missing, and now I knew I couldn't live without.

Epilogue

WINTER HAD firmly set in, and the wind whistled outside the barn doors. For the first time, I saddled Storm with the intent of trying to actually ride him. I had saddled him before, and he had even let me sit on his back while Scarborough held a lead. But today the plan was to take him into one of the paddocks and see if he'd let me just ride.

"Do you really think he isn't going to bolt and throw you?" Scarborough asked. "He's a good horse, and we don't need to ride him ever."

"I know. But I think he's ready, and Storm is happy now." I led Storm out of the barn and into the paddock. He was relaxed and tossed his head idly. When Storm was in the center of the paddock, I put the reins over his head and then held my breath as I slowly mounted him and settled into the saddle. Storm stood still, and I waited to see how he was going to react. "Let's walk." I nudged him forward, and Storm began to walk.

"Isn't he a thing of beauty," Mom said as she approached the rail and leaned against it, nestled in her thick blue coat.

"Yes, he is, Mom."

"It just goes to show that even the most damaged and hurt of us can thrive with love and care," Scarborough said.

I smiled, patting Storm and praising him even as I wondered if Scarborough was talking about Storm or himself. Maybe both. Scarborough had thrived over the fall and into the winter. He and I were negotiating to buy the land next to his place, and in the spring, the plan was to add more cattle and to hire a few hands to help with the increased work. I had already moved a lot of my things into Scarborough's house, and the hired hands would live at my place. Things were working out on most fronts, and the others… we were working through those together, no shutouts. Scarborough, for the most part, had left his shell behind, and I let him work through things on his own—within reason.

Storm and I continued walking around the paddock, just going at a leisurely pace. This was so much more than I had ever hoped for with him. The way I had first seen him, I'd had my doubts, but Storm had proven me wrong. He was a lot stronger and had more heart than I had first given him credit for.

As I made a second circuit, I saw Dad join Mom and Scarborough, watching the two of us. "He's really stunning." Dad pulled out his phone and took some pictures, and damned if Storm didn't stop like he was posing for the camera. It turned out the horse was a ham.

After ten minutes, I pulled Storm to a stop and carefully dismounted, walked him around, and then led him back to the barn. "You were amazing, boy," I told him, talking gently as I got his gear off and giving him an extra portion of oats.

"That was awesome," Scarborough said as I closed the stall door, and then I was engulfed in his arms. "Your dad just told me that come spring, he has eight fillies signed up for Storm, and that's in addition to the ones he wants to breed, as well as our own."

I was thrilled at his excitement. "That's wonderful," I told him, cupping his cheeks. "Maybe you should buy horses at auction more often." I slowly closed the distance between us, drawing him ever nearer.

"Maybe you and I should consider ourselves lucky and not press our luck." Scarborough tugged me tight as the chill wound around us for a second before being banished by the heat that

Scarborough generated in me. I leaned forward and captured his lips, tasting his heat and a touch of the fresh air on his tongue.

"True. I was lucky enough to get you. That's more than enough for me."

ANDREW GREY is the author of more than one hundred works of Contemporary Gay Romantic fiction. After twenty-seven years in corporate America, he has now settled down in Central Pennsylvania with his husband, Dominic, and his laptop. An interesting ménage. Andrew grew up in western Michigan with a father who loved to tell stories and a mother who loved to read them. Since then he has lived throughout the country and traveled throughout the world. He is a recipient of the RWA Centennial Award, has a master's degree from the University of Wisconsin–Milwaukee, and now writes full-time. Andrew's hobbies include collecting antiques, gardening, and leaving his dirty dishes anywhere but in the sink (particularly when writing). He considers himself blessed with an accepting family, fantastic friends, and the world's most supportive and loving partner. Andrew currently lives in beautiful, historic Carlisle, Pennsylvania.

Email: andrewgrey@comcast.net
Website: www.andrewgreybooks.com

andrew grey

Catch

of a Lifetime

Some moments happen once in a lifetime, and you have to catch them and hold on tight.

Arty Reynolds chased his dream to Broadway, but after his father is injured, he must return to the small fishing community where he grew up, at least until his dad is back on his feet.

Jamie Wilson fled his family farm, but failed to achieve real independence. Arty is hiring for a trip on the gulf, and it'll get Jamie one step closer to his goal.

Neither man plans to stay in Florida long-term, neither is looking for love, and they're both blown away by the passion that sparks between them. But on a fishing boat, there's little privacy to see where their feelings might lead. Passion builds like a storm until they reach land, where they also learn they share a common dream. The lives they both long for could line up perfectly, as long as they can weather the strain on their new romance when only one of them may get a chance at their dream.

www.dreampsinnerpress.com

HEARTWARD

He doesn't know that home is where his heart will be….

Firefighter Tyler Banik has seen his share of adventure while working disaster relief with the Red Cross. But now that he's adopted Abey, he's ready to leave the danger behind and put down roots. That means returning to his hometown—where the last thing he anticipates is falling for his high school nemesis.

Alan Pettaprin isn't the boy he used to be. As a business owner and council member, he's working hard to improve life in Scottville for everyone. Nobody is more surprised than Alan when Tyler returns, but he's glad. For him, it's a chance to set things right. Little does he guess he and Tyler will find the missing pieces of themselves in each other. Old rivalries are left in the ashes, passion burns bright, and the possibility for a future together stretches in front of them….

But not everyone in town is glad to see Tyler return….

www.dreamspinnerpress.com

A high-stakes case of industrial espionage ties them together, but before they can pursue their attraction, they must find out who's pulling the strings.

Devon Donaldson doesn't know how a folio of stolen corporate secrets found its way into his bag, and certainly can't think of anyone who'd want to frame him. The trouble is, he has to convince Powers McPherson.

Devon's firm hired Powers to investigate the theft of a new banking system, and so far Devon is his only lead. While Powers's gut tells him Devon is innocent, he has no intention of letting Devon out of his sight… for more than one reason. Working together to get Devon's life back leads to feelings far beyond cooperation. But before they can act on them, they need to find the group of thieves intent on ruining Devon's reputation.

www.dreamspinnerpress.com

2019 ADVENT ANTHOLOGY
Homemade
for the Holidays

Andrew Grey
SWEET
ANTICIPATION

Greg Hansen's pregnant sister is on bed rest, so it falls to Greg to finalize the arrangements for her best friend's bachelorette party. Little does he know he's in for a sweet surprise. When he arrives at the bakery recommended to him, he comes face to face with the man he never should've let get away—Rhys Denning.

Rhys's business is booming with the holidays approaching, so he can't agree to cater the party without help—and that means Greg getting his hands dirty in the kitchen, where the two reconnect over sugar, spice, holiday goodies of all kinds, and even some penis-shaped baguettes! But the most satisfying treat might be the second chance they never thought they'd get.

www.dreamspinnerpress.com

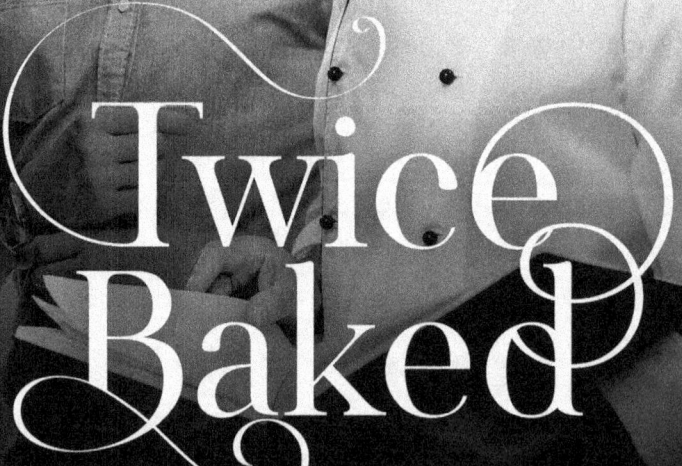

Twice Baked

ANDREW GREY

When the pickiest eater in America is tapped to judge a cooking competition along with his chef ex-boyfriend, will it be a recipe for a second chance… or disaster?

Luke Walker's humor about foods he can't stand made him an internet celebrity and his blog, The Pickiest Eater in America, a huge hit. He plans to bring that same lighthearted comedy to the show—but he won't be the only host.

Meyer Thibodeaux might be a famous chef, but he's solemn, uptight, and closeted. He's also Luke's ex. As different as they are, the sparks between Luke and Meyer never really went out, and as they work together, each begins to see the other in a new light, and the passion between them reignites, hot as ever. But secrets, gossip, and rumors on the set could sour their reunion.

www.dreamspinnerpress.com

www.ingramcontent.com/pod-product-compliance
Lightning Source LLC
Chambersburg PA
CBHW060059260626
47160CB00005B/1721